Her Outback Paradise

Annie Seaton

ANNIE SEATON

Her Outback Paradise
Copyright © September 2019, Annie Seaton.

NOTE: This book is a work of fiction. The names, characters, places, and incidents are products of the writer's imagination or have been used fictitiously and are not to be construed as real. Any resemblance to persons, living or dead, actual events, locale or organisations is entirely coincidental.
ISBN 978-0-6450584-9-9

Cover creation: Annie Seaton.

If you would like to meet the McDougal family in the stories before Her Outback Paradise:

Her Outback Playboy - Jenni's story

Her Outback Protector - Don's story

Her Outback Haven - Dane's story

are available now in print and e-books.

See Annie's books page for details:

https://www.annieseaton.net/second-chance-bay-series.html

See Annie's online store to purchase in print:

https://www.annieseaton.net/store.html

Acknowledgments

A special thank you to my wonderful editor and critique partner, Susanne Bellamy,
and my eagle-eyed proof-reader, Roby Aiken.

ANNIE SEATON

Chapter One

'Omigod, omigod, omigod!' Sara Sweeney squealed and twirled in the tiny kitchen of her granny flat, and then squealed again when the phone fell off the kitchen countertop, landing with a crash on the faded pink tiles. 'Sorry, Caro. Are you still there?'

Sara picked up the phone and pressed it to her ear but all she could hear was static. Hurrying to her bedroom she tipped the contents of her handbag onto the bed looking for her mobile.

'Damn, damn, where is it?' As Sara spotted it, the ACDC song she'd downloaded for her ringtone filled the small room, and she grabbed for the phone.

'Caro? Sorry, I forgot I was on the landline and I dropped it and I've killed the phone. Did you say what I thought you did?'

The calm tones of her friend's voice assured her that she had heard her right the first time. Sara flopped onto the bed and put her hand on her chest. 'That is awesome! When did you make up your mind?'

'About three o'clock this morning. I figured there was no point staying here.'

'True.'

'My contract is coming to an end, and well—as you know—it's not really a place I want to be.'

'I know, sweets. Even though the Barossa Valley is a beautiful part of Australia, you've done it tough here.' Sara jiggled her feet on the end of the bed. 'Oh. My. God. I can't believe it. You're coming with me to Second Chance Bay! You know how excited I am about finally going home.'

'I do, but slow down. I'm just going there to check it out first. I haven't agreed to the contract yet. Sar?' Caro's voice was quiet. 'I want to ask a favour.'

'Shoot, love.'

'You don't start your job up there in the medical centre for a few weeks, do you?'

'That's right, I have a wonderful month of no work after I finish up with Roger the Dodger.'

There was silence at the other end, and Sara waited. Caro was her exact opposite: calm, considered and quiet, while Sara knew that she rushed at life. Like a bull in a china shop, as her grandmother had often told her when Sara was growing up. It would be so good to see Nan when she got back to the Bay. It had been way too long; it would be so good to be home at Second Chance Bay.

'I was thinking about taking a road trip,' Caro finally said. 'I'd like to take my own vehicle up to

Queensland. It sounds as though some of the roads up there are rough.'

'You can say that again,' Sara replied. 'You mean a road trip up to Second Chance Bay?'

'Yes, how would you feel about travelling up with me by road instead of flying up? I was thinking about taking the longer route. Taking a trip up through Alice Springs and stopping to have a look at Uluru and Kata Tjuta on the way.'

'Of course. I'd love to. It'll be great fun. And I've never seen the Red Centre either. I've always flown out to Mt Isa to go home.'

'Excellent.'

'It's a long way though. Are you sure you want to be on the road for that long?'

'It's over three thousand kilometres, but you know what, Sar? It's about time I got out of my rut and did something exciting.'

'And I'm happy to share the driving.' Sara jumped off the bed and crossed to the window and looked out at the gloomy sky. 'Where will we stay? There's not many motels along the way.'

'Well, speaking of adventures. I was thinking about taking a couple of swags and some camping gear. What do you think?'

'I think it sounds like a top idea! When will we leave?'

'As soon as my contract is up.'

'When do you finish at the practice? Same time as me?' Sara went to her desk and looked at the calendar that was propped up on her small dressing table.

'Yes, same as you. This Friday. Roger wanted to take us both to dinner on Saturday night to farewell us both, but I told him we would be gone. I hope that was okay. Even if you don't come with me, it gives you an out.'

'Good. The less time I spend in his company the better!'

'I was thinking about leaving as soon as possible, and take my time and have a good look around.'

'Well then, we need to get organised. I told Mrs Digby that I'd be leaving the flat early next week, but luckily I haven't booked any flights yet.'

'It's going to be fun, isn't it?' Caroline's voice was quiet, and Sara frowned. It *would* be fun, and it would do Caro a power of good. She already had some ideas about how to cheer her up when they arrived in Sara's hometown. Sara crossed her fingers that she could make it so welcoming that Caro would take the contract she'd been offered as resident doctor at the medical practice. Sara was starting there as receptionist and clinic sister in a month's time. Sara crossed her fingers that she could make it so welcoming that Caro would take the contract she'd been offered as resident doctor at the medical practice. Sara was starting there as receptionist and clinic sister in a month's time. It would be *great* to have Caro in the practice. While she'd loved working as receptionist for Dr Rose before she'd moved away, he could be a bit of a stick in the mud when it came to making the workplace a bit of fun.

He was middle-aged and devoted to his career. On the rare occasion that he smiled, he wasn't a bad-looking man. Dr Rose kept himself fit and trim and as the local table tennis champion these days, according to Nan.

'I think we need to get together as soon as we can and start planning this trip.' Sara looked at the mess of the small amount of packing she'd done. At least if she was in a vehicle, the packing would be way easier. A couple of boxes would hold what she wanted to take home, and she'd leave the rest for Mrs Digby, her landlady. She was going home to stay after eight years away.

Home. Finally.

'A good idea. What are you doing now?' Caro's voice interrupted her planning.

Sara grinned. 'I was supposed to be packing, but let's meet somewhere for coffee and get this trip organised.'

##

Sara was surprised when Caro suggested that they go out to one of the vineyards outside the small town of Tanunda where they both lived. Caroline was not usually one to socialise, but Sara was already planning to work on that when they arrived at Second Chance Bay. The trip would be a great opportunity to get to know Caro better, and what she liked to do. Also, Sara knew there was some mystery in the doctor's past. She always seemed very sad, and maybe moving to Second Chance Bay would give her a new perspective. Sara had never asked what had happened; maybe the trip would lead to some heart-to-heart conversations.

She grinned and thought of her grandmother.

Yes, Nan, I'm still Mrs Fixit, she thought. *I'm just no good at fixing myself.*

'I'll pick you up, and I'll drive because I'm on call at the hospital tonight. They do woodfired pizza and red wine out at the Italian one,' Caro said.

'Sounds perfect!'

Half an hour later, Sara slipped her warm coat on over her jeans and jumper and ran out to Caroline's four-wheel drive. A slight shower had left the grass wet, and she shivered as she opened the door. The heater was on in the car and it was toasty warm.

'Mm, bliss. A much better way to spend a Sunday afternoon than packing,' Sara said as she secured the seatbelt. 'I can't wait to get back to the tropics.'

Caro nodded. 'It is.' Her cheeks were pink, her eyes bright and she looked happier than she usually did. She looked curiously at Sara. 'You really are excited about going back to your hometown, aren't you?'

'I'm excited about going home.'

'What's so special about it?'

Sara considered her words carefully. She wanted Caro to take the position at the local clinic, and she didn't want to discourage her. At the same time she didn't want to build up any false expectations, and have Caro disappointed when she arrived at the Bay.

Sara was receptionist and clinic nurse at the local medical practice and had befriended Caro when she had arrived there as a locum twelve months ago. The doctor Caro had replaced hadn't returned, and she'd ended up signing a twelve-month contract. Dr Roger Dolman—Roger the Dodger to Sara—was a difficult boss, but Sara knew it wasn't her place to warn prospective staff that the work environment could be unpleasant. She'd learned to cope with it, and it was a job in a pleasant area that paid the bills. It had always been a temporary stop for Sara as she worked her way home to Second Chance Bay.

The vineyards were a great place to live and there was always plenty to do and see, but nothing compared to the outback paradise of home.

Over the months, and to her credit, Caro had handled Roger well, managing to fend off his advances—never inappropriate, but always on the edge—without jeopardising her job. Dr Dolman knew how hard it was to get doctors in the country and was on his best behaviour—most of the time. Caro and Sara had formed an alliance, and the crusty old bachelor boss had taken the hint and stopped asking each of them out.

'It's a quaint little town on the Gulf of Carpentaria.'

'Quaint?'

'Maybe not quaint like the pretty little towns down here in the Barossa Valley. Maybe unique is a better word than quaint.'

'You have me intrigued.'

'It's a very small town, but in winter it fills up with retirees and tourists from the southern states. They chase the warmth. Our climate is fabulous.'

'Hot in the summer though?' Caro indicated to turn onto the main road.

'We have air conditioners.' Sara flicked a sideways glance at Caro. 'I'm so looking forward to this trip. It's a great idea to drive up.'

Caro nodded. 'I figured it was a way to have a holiday and see the country. I'm so pleased you've agreed to come with me.' She changed back a gear as they slowed behind a truck. The vineyards were bare and grey beneath the heavy cloud, but Sara had lived in the Barossa Valley for two years after—

Nope, don't go there.

The car hummed smoothly along the bitumen and soon they turned into the little boutique winery south of town. 'I figured if I get called into the hospital while we're eating it's close enough for you to get a taxi home.' Caro parked the car and reached over to the back seat for her jacket.

Sara shivered again while she waited for Caro to button up her jacket. The wind had picked up and it felt like it was blowing off the Antarctic. 'You won't need that up at the Bay,' she said with a grin.

'I'm looking forward to heading north,' Caro said. They walked into the cosy restaurant and snagged a small table next to the open fire.

'Coffee or wine first?' Sara glanced at her watch. 'It's after three.'

Caro smiled. 'It's a winery. I can have one glass. I need it to warm up.'

Soon they were settled, and Sara leaned back in her chair and looked at the bright flames crackling in the hearth. 'That's about the only thing I'll miss about here. I do love to sit in front of a fire.' She chuckled. 'Sometimes in winter when we have a barbie at home, we light a bonfire, but that's as close as we get.'

Caro lifted her wine glass and the firelight caught the ruby red liquid.

'And the afternoons at the vineyards,' Sara added. 'I've been to some great concerts since I've been here.'

'Tell me how you ended up in the Barossa Valley. It's a long way from the Gulf of Carpentaria.'

Sara lifted her wine and watched as it caught the firelight too. 'The warts and all story? I guess we've got time.'

As she leaned forward to begin her story, a shadow fell across the table and Sara looked up.

'Well, blow me down. Sara Sweeney, as I live and breathe!'

'Maisie! What a surprise. I thought you'd be up in the Bay.' Sara smiled at the older woman. Maisie had been a regular visitor to Second Chance Bay every winter for as long as Sara could remember.

'I came here from Melbourne on a bus trip with some other old boilers. I'm flying up to the Bay in a couple of weeks. I leave my van up there these days. I'm getting too old and doddery to tow it all the way from the bottom to the top of the country. I thought it was you, Sara. What on earth are you doing down here?'

'I live here,' Sara replied.

'Married? Kids? Partner?' She flicked a curious glance at Caro, and Sara bit back a smile.

'No. None of that. I'm a career girl these days.' She turned to Caro. 'Maisie, this is my friend and colleague, Caroline. Caro, this is Maisie who's known me since I was a kid.'

'And a pretty kid, she was.' Maisie shook her head. 'You broke young Mattie's heart when you left the Bay, Sara.'

Despite her chuckle, something thick lodged in Sara's throat. 'I'm sure it wasn't a broken heart.'

Maisie nodded. 'Oh yes, it was. The poor boy is still single.'

Sara swallowed and forced a smile to her face; for a moment going home lost its appeal. 'I'm sure Matthew McDougal is still enjoying life as much as he ever was. And the poor *boy* can't be that far off forty. I'm thirty-five.'

Caro smiled over at Sara. 'Sounds like you've got a reason to go home?'

Sara pulled a face at her. 'Don't you start.' She looked up at Maisie. 'Caro and I are about to take a road trip. I'll be back at the Bay in a month. I'm coming home to work at the medical surgery and Caro might be going to work with Dr Rose.'

'You're a doctor, love?' Maisie stared at Caroline and Sara could see that she had gone up in her estimation.

'I am, and Sara has enticed me to visit the Bay.'

'Best place in the world.' Maisie's blue-rinsed hair bounced as she nodded. 'I'll see you both soon, then. Nice to meet you, Doctor.'

Sara giggled as Maisie went back to her table. 'You've hit the big time but be warned. Second Chance Bay will know all about you by the time we arrive now that Maisie knows you're coming.'

Caro leaned forward. 'Now tell me about this guy whose heart you broke.'

Chapter Two

Two weeks later

Matt McDougal opened the door of the rusted refrigerator in the small kitchenette. It had sat at the back of the tiny room in the family fish co-op since he was a kid. He'd opened that fridge probably five times a day for the past fifteen years, ever since their father had died. His accountant's brain kicked in as he reached in and pulled out the carton of milk.

Five times a day, multiplied by three hundred and sixty days—the family business only closed on public holidays—multiplied by fifteen years. He closed the door harder than he usually would and the milk slopped out of the carton onto his hand.

Damn.

His already-strange mood deteriorated further. 27,000 times he'd probably opened the door of that bloody old Kelvinator fridge. The jug boiled and he poured the boiling water onto his coffee bag.

Why did he have to be the one who worried about money?

He could have bought a new fridge anytime over the past couple of years, and why was he letting it worry him so much today?

Jake's flash charter boats, Matt's little brother, Donny's, new luxury boat out in the Kimberley rivers, and his other brother, Dane's, fancy new lodge up in the Gulf probably all had good coffee machines, and here he was in a run-down old building with a coffee bag, boiling an old plastic jug.

The rest of his family were settled—in great relationships and financially secure—and he'd let himself get stuck in this old building, worrying about the dollars when there was no longer any need to. It was time to stop burying himself in the business and do something about it.

But what did he want to do? The one woman he might have settled with had left him—he'd made sure of that—and up until now he'd been content to stay looking after the finances of the family fish co-op, and then as his siblings expanded their interests into other areas, he'd naturally overseen the finances.

Jake was married to Matt's sister, Jenni, and Matt adored little his niece, Leni, and now there was his nephew, Callen, a relatively new addition to the family. Donny and Claire were working over in the Kimberleys in Western Australia, and Dane and

Nicole were up at Staaten River adding two more lodges to their thriving business.

Matt winced as the steam from the jug burned his wrist, and when the coffee was a decent strength, he lifted the bag out and threw it in the sink. As he walked back into this office, the bell above the door tinkled, indicating a customer and he turned and headed out into the shop.

Not only did he look after the accounts for the family businesses, but he was also expected to serve bloody prawns.

'Bloody Nora, Matthew! Is the milk in that coffee sour? It must be by the look on your face.'

Matt smiled, and his smile was genuine, despite his bad mood. He put his coffee on the counter and hurried around to the other side.

'Hey there, Miss Maisie. You're back so it must be winter down south. Give me a hug!'

The older woman hugged him back. 'Bloody heck, Matthew, you're getting more like your father every year.'

'Maybe I look like him, but I'm not like him.' Matt's voice was terse as his bad mood come rushing back.

'Of course, you're not. But you sure have a look of him. How's your Mum?'

'She's well. She and Rick are away in Europe.'

'Oh, the lucky duck, but she does deserve it after all she went through.'

'She does.' Matt didn't need reminding of that and he frowned as he observed the curly blue-rinsed head of hair. 'Now, what's this I hear about you moving to the best site in the caravan park.'

Maisie pouted and her gravelly voice rasped out. 'Now who the friggin' heck told you? There's no secrets in this bloody town!'

Matt tapped the side of his nose. Maisie was a character and her language was often as blue as her hair. 'I went over there looking for you last week. I thought you'd be due to arrive soon. Kev told me that he'd put you on the site at the end of Toorak Lane. The one with the best view of the water.'

'Yep. Old Sheila McIntyre went into a home after her Jimmy carked it.'

Matt swallowed a smile. 'I'm sorry to hear that.'

'Gawd, I'm not,' Maisie said. 'She was a right bitch and she thought she was the queen of the park. She'd only been coming up for twenty-five years. I beat her by two years, but I still got relegated down to Dunrootin' Lane when my Reg died.'

'Ah, the social politics of a caravan park. But I guess you're the new queen now?' Matt reached for his coffee.

Her nod was definite and her smile smug. 'I sure as tootin' am. We're going to get rid of that stupid bridge game they were playing and go back to a decent round of poker every afternoon.'

Matt chuckled. 'Maisie, it's so good to have you back.'

'So why were you looking for me, love? You need a hand in the shop?'

Maisie had helped out in the shop when she came up from Melbourne for as long as Matt could remember. She was great with the grey nomies, and they usually ended up spending more than they intended.

'If you're free.' He grinned and winked. 'Although you're now a woman of power . . .'

'Don't be bloody stupid. Go and make me a coffee and I'll put an apron on. Might as well start now. You look like you need cheering up.' She looked around. 'Are you here by yourself these days? Is that why you were looking so bloody miserable when I walked in? Where's that pretty young girl who was here last winter? I had high hopes there.'

'What girl?' Matt took a sip of his coffee. 'I don't remember.'

'Well, I guess you didn't score then.' Maisie's husky laugh rumbled through the shop. 'Or if you did, it wasn't memorable.'

21

Matt shook his head. 'You're incorrigible. It's good to have you back, Maisie. How many hours work do you want?'

'I'll just go outside and have a ciggie before I start. I'll have a think about the hours.' She pushed the door open and the bell jangled again. 'White with two sugars if you've forgotten, and none of that fancy bag stuff. A heaped teaspoon of International Roast'll do me.'

Matt grinned as he went back into the kitchen and flicked the jug on. He reached up and pulled out the tin of coffee that had been in the cupboard since last year when Maisie had worked in the co-op and was pleased that it hadn't solidified. He'd get a fresh one when he went to the shop. Maisie's two major pastimes were coffee and her beloved ciggies; it was a wonder she was still healthy.

By the time Matt had made the hot drink as directed and gone back into the shop, she was behind the counter kitted out in the yellow plastic apron; the smell of cigarettes had wafted in with her.

'Thank you, sweets. You're a treasure,' she said. 'Now tell me all about the family and what everyone's up to.'

Matt filled Maisie in on where everyone was, and that Mum and Rick were due back at the end of winter. 'They've been overseas a couple of months.

Mum said she wanted to do one of those river cruises.'

Maisie nodded. 'Best thing she ever did was hooking up with that Rick. He was a good catch. If I'd been a few years younger when Reg died . . .'

Matt tried not to choke on his coffee. He swallowed and smiled at her. 'I'm sure you would have given Mum a run for her money.'

'That I would.' Maisie reached under the counter and pulled out a fresh packet of the white paper that they wrapped the prawns in. 'You go and get back to work in the office. I'll take over out here.'

As Matt turned to go back to his desk, she called out to him. 'Oh, I forgot to tell you who I bumped into a couple of weeks ago. Guess!'

Matt shook his head. 'I have no idea.'

'The new doctor who's going to work with Doc Rose. I'd heard the doc was thinking of getting a second doctor in town.'

'I heard that too. It's been busy since the mine expanded. There's new families arriving in town each week. I know he was worried about getting someone to come to the Bay. Anyone from down south thinks we're too far away from everything.'

'Best place in Australia if you ask me. If it wasn't so bloody hot in the wet season, I'd move up here for good.' She looked at him intently. 'And you'll never guess who's coming with the new doc.'

'Who?' Matt was already thinking about what he was going to do first. Jake had asked him to get some prices on some new fishing reels for *Moonshine*, and Dane was waiting for him to mail the latest building quote for the new cabin at the lodge up to him.

'She's coming home.'

Matt screwed his nose up. 'Sorry, you've lost me.'

Maisie shook her head and spoke slowly. 'Sara Sweeney. She's coming home.'

Matt stood still and a strange feeling washed over him. For a moment he didn't say anything, and he tried to clear his expression because he knew how savvy Maisie was.

'Sara? She's with the new doctor?' The thought of Sara moving back to town with a partner did not sit comfortably with Matt, even though he had no right to feel that way.

He and Sara Sweeney had had a pretty hot and heavy relationship when she'd lived here, and he'd known that Sara wanted to settle down. She'd been after the engagement, the white wedding, the kids and the house and the whole thing, but that was the one thing he hadn't been able to give her.

Eventually, she'd got sick of waiting for him to settle down, and moved to Adelaide. It had been the best thing for both of them.

'She was with the new doctor. They were planning a Thelma and Louise.'

Matt scratched his head. 'Maisie, what are you talking about? What's a Thelma and Louise?'

'Honestly Matt, you're such a typical man. You don't listen. It's a road trip.'

'Oh,' he said, none the wiser.

'I saw them in a winery.'

'Who? Thelma and Louise? Who are they?' Matt stared at her.

Maybe it wasn't such a good idea to hire Maisie. What would she be now? Heading for her late seventies. Was this the first sign of dementia kicking in?

'You think I've lost the plot, don't you?' Maisie laughed as she looked at him. 'I was on a bus trip to the Barossa Valley and they were there at a winery. Sara and the new doc are driving up from Adelaide, like Thelma and Louise in that movie.'

'Oh. It's Sara who's coming home then. For a visit? Or to stay?' Matt didn't know how he felt about that. But he knew it would be hard to see Sara with a partner.

'Does she have any kids?'

'Who? The new doctor or Sara?

Matt frowned. 'The new doctor is a woman?'

'Yes. Sheesh, it'd be hard for a guy to do a Thelma and Louise.' Maisie put her hands on her hips. 'I've got the DVD in the caravan. I'll lend it to you.' They both looked up as the bell above the door tinkled and three couples walked in. 'You go and work, I'll look after the customers.'

'Thanks, Mais. You're a great help.'

'No wuckers, mate.'

Matt rolled his eyes and walked to his small office as Maisie greeted the customers. 'What can I do for you, love?'

He sat at his desk for a long time before he turned his computer on. Sara Sweeney coming home raised a whole heap of memories. Funny that he'd been thinking about her before Maisie had arrived.

A tiny little burst of happiness settled in his chest. Maybe she was home to stay?

Matt shook his head and pushed the excitement away.

It didn't matter how long Sara was coming home for; it wouldn't make any difference to how he felt. Matt didn't intend to settle down with anyone.

Ever.

Not even the woman he'd once been in love with.

Chapter Three

'And you just upped and left?' Caro said as she slowed down behind the van ahead of them as they approached the Northern Territory border. Being on the road and spending many hours in a car together had moved Sara and Caro's professional relationship into a friendship. Even though they'd worked together for a year and been out for coffee a few times, Sara hadn't known much about Caro's past, and she hadn't shared her story yet. There'd been a few hints, but Sara hadn't pressed her. If Caro wanted her to know, she would share when she was ready.

In the two weeks on the road, Sara had shared her story with Caroline.

Well, half of it.

Caro had been curious the afternoon they'd met to plan the trip and had asked about Matt after Maisie moved away from their table.

Sara had been vague. The first of her two big hurts still sat deep within and seeing Maisie had raised a lot of memories. Twice in her life, she'd been rejected, and it had taken her to thirty-five to regain her confidence and have faith in herself. She hid her lack of confidence behind a ditzy exterior and always put on a happy face. No one would ever have guessed that a shy woman with low self-confidence hid beneath those colourful out-there outfits, crazy red curly hair and loud jokes.

'I did. I could see us going on like that for years. Matt was happy with his life the way it was, and his brothers were the same. They lived for their fishing'—Sara chuckled— 'I mean Dane and Donny did. Matt got too seasick to go out on the water. He ran the business side of things, and I guess he probably still does. Three bachelors, ripe for the picking but too involved in their business to have any time for anything else.'

'And you wanted different things?'

Sara nodded as Caro pulled out to overtake the long caravan in front of them. She waited until they were around it and pulled into the lane ahead. 'I did. Back in those days, I thought I wanted marriage and kids, but I guess Matt did me a favour. I guess we just fell out of love—or I did anyway.' She crossed her fingers. 'We were probably too young.'

Caro flicked her a glance. 'I thought it was only a few years ago. You couldn't have been that young.'

'True. It was eight years ago.' Sara pulled a face. 'After I left and I thought about it, I knew that it wasn't that. I mean, I was twenty-seven, and Matt was thirty. When I pushed, he said we had plenty of time.'

'And you could hear the biological clock ticking?'

'I could. And there were so many girlie flicks out then about that. I guess I let them bother me too much. When I raised it with Matt, I knew I was wasting my time and he didn't want me, so I left the same week, rather than wait and get hurt.'

'He told you that he didn't want you?' Caro reached over and turned the music volume down as she waited for Sara to answer.

'No, not in so many words. I knew he was making excuses, so I decided to go.'

'What did he say?'

'I didn't tell him I was going. I haven't seen him or talked to him since I left.'

'And he's still single?'

Sara shrugged. 'Apparently. But listen, Caro, don't go getting any ideas. I'm over Matt McDougal and he did me a favour. He really is a lovely guy. I wasn't the right woman for him.' She looked sideways at Caro. 'Now if he's still single . . . maybe . . .'

'You'd have another go?'

'No! I meant you might like to meet him.'

Carolyn shook her head emphatically. 'No chance. I'm up here to work and—'

She bit her lip as she focused on the road.

'And?' Sara asked

'And to recover from a similar experience.' Caro laughed. 'I think our experience with the opposite sex went a long way to helping us deal so firmly with Roger.'

'He was harmless. It was his persistence that was annoying.'

Caroline shook her head again. 'No, Sara. It's never harmless. We could cope with his insistent behaviour because we had maturity and experience on our side. Imagine if someone with no self-confidence started working for him.'

'I don't have that much self-confidence, you know.' Sara looked down at her hands clenched on her lap. 'A couple of years ago I had the same experience as I did with Matt, with another guy and it left me pretty fragile. I made up my mind when I moved to Tanunda, I was meant to stay single. For a long time, I believed I wasn't good enough for anyone. And now I've accepted my time's passed. I'm happy being by myself. My confidence is back, and I'm looking forward to going home.'

'Sure there's no chance of rekindling that relationship? Maisie said you broke his heart.'

The sound that came from Sara's mouth was a cross between a snort and a laugh. 'Now that I don't believe. Now I've shared with you, you can tell me your story.'

Caro changed back a gear and slowed down as a huge road train appeared on the horizon. 'God, I hate those big trucks. They shake the car.' She was quiet until the truck with the triple trailer passed them. 'Are you happy to stop for the night at the roadhouse across the border? Or do you want to drive for a while?'

'Let's stop. I had a look at the map and it's a long way before the next roadhouse. Almost to the Uluru turnoff.' Sara was sick of being in the car, although the prospect of another night of rolling out her swag on red dirt didn't appeal greatly either.

'Okay, we're almost there.' Caro glanced across at Sara. 'And over a wine I'll tell you my story. It's not so different to yours, but I was a lot older. My biological clock had already run out.'

They were quiet as each was lost in their thoughts for the next half hour. Talking about Matt had helped Sara realise that she was over him. It had taken a long time, and then when she'd met Jeff, she'd believed she was ready for another relationship. She bit back the sigh that rose in her chest. She thought it had been hard when Matt had rejected her. The fiasco with Jeff in Adelaide had turned her off relationships for life. She wasn't destined to be a wife and mother; it had taken some getting used to, but she'd accepted her life as a single woman, and she'd learned to be happy.

Sara reached over and turned the music up again. 'I think we need some happy music.'

They both laughed when the next song came on.

'Who needs the Bee Gees singing about being alone!' She searched her phone. 'Let's have some Pink!'

***

Ever since Maisie had told him that Sara was on the way home—and she didn't have a partner—Matt had been restless. On the first Saturday in July, after hectic days in the co-op and hectic nights trying to get the tax for four businesses up to scratch, he was pleased when Jenni arrived at the shop just before closing with Leni holding one hand, and a pram being pushed with the other.

'Uncle Mattie.' The little girl ran through the door with a squeal and launched herself into Matt's open arms. 'We's having a barbie. Can you come?'

Matt squeezed her and dropped a kiss on the top of the blonde curls. 'I sure can. I need feeding. Your poor Uncle Matt has been working so hard he forgot to eat.'

Jenni pulled a face at him. 'More likely you were too lazy to cook. Besides Jake said he saw you having dinner at the pub the other night.'

Matt shook his head. 'One night at the pub and I'm the talk of the Bay. Jeez, you've gotta love this town.' He ruffled Leni's hair as he put her down. 'You tell your Mummy to be nice to Uncle Matt. I've been working my butt off, Jen.'

'And you think we've all been having a holiday?' I haven't seen Jake for fourteen days straight. He had two back-to-back charters.' Jenni folded her arms. 'Do you want to come over for dinner or are you too busy being the family martyr?' Her tone was sharp, and it hurt. Jenni had always been the one to tell it how it was.

Matt ran his hand through his hair; he needed a haircut. 'Of course, I'll come and I'm sorry for being a grumpy bum. It's been a busy week. I didn't get the Boyle girl to come in after school because Maisie's back in town and was going to give me some hours, but she only turned up once. I've been flat out in the shop.'

'Maisie's in the hospital.'

'What?' Matt stared. 'Is she okay?'

Jenni nodded. 'I'm sorry. I thought you knew. Lurline on the desk at the hospital said she'd call you, because Maisie asked her to let you know she couldn't work for a few days.'

'I would have gone straight over if I'd known. 'Matt glanced at his watch. 'Is she okay? What happened?'

33

'She had a fall.' Jenni put her hand up. 'Don't worry. It wasn't her age or anything. Apparently, someone had dug a hole at the side of the amenities block and hadn't roped it off. Maisie tripped and fell in the dark. She's okay, but they were keeping her in for a few days until the swelling in her ankle went down seeing she's by herself in the park.'

'Poor old love. I wonder if it's too late to get flowers at IGA? I'll go over and see her after I close up.'

'That'd be nice. Give her my love. And Matt, if you go to IGA can you get me a big tub of coleslaw for tonight, please? The others are all in town.'

'What others?'

Jenni shook her head. 'For someone who supposedly runs the business, you don't have a clue! Your brothers are both in town. And Claire and Nicole too.'

Matt's face lit up in a smile. 'That's great. It's ages since we've all been together.'

He looked up at the clock. 'I'm going to close up now. What time are they arriving?'

'They'll be here soon.'

'Right. I'll go across river and have a shower and then see Maisie on the way to your place.'

Jenni turned as she reached the door. 'And one more thing. Tonight is a family occasion. No business talk. Okay?'

He nodded. 'I can do that. I'm looking forward to catching up with the boys.'

'If Jake gets home in time.' Jenni held the door open with her hip as she ushered Leni in front of the pram.

'You okay, sis?'

'I'm fine. I'll see you in a while. Don't forget the coleslaw.'

Matt would never admit it to anyone, but he'd always been a little bit jealous of his brother-in-law. Jake Jones had travelled and lived in France and came back to Second Chance Bay. By then he had come back mature, experienced and very wealthy.

Matt felt guilty—Jake was an all-round nice guy. But Jenni was his baby sister, and they'd been close. Now that she was with Jake, he and Jenni weren't as close as they'd been growing up, but he still watched out for her.

And now that Dane and Donny had their partners, Matt spent a lot of time home alone in the old family house. That unfamiliar restlessness tugged at him.

Maybe it was time for a change.

He nodded as he got ready to lock up the shop. It was time for him to leave town. There was a big wide world out there and it was time to go and find it.

And if he wasn't here, he couldn't be tempted by Sara Sweeney.

Chapter Four

The smell of steak and onions enticed Matt as he pushed open the gate of Jenni and Jake's new house on the point north of town. Jake had come back to the Bay, having made his fortune on the Cote d'Azur, and then made peace with the family, married Jenni and gone into partnership in the charter side of the business.

Jake and Jenni had been high school sweethearts, but Matt and Jenni's father had caused trouble between them and Jake had fled town not long after he'd left school. Not the only trouble the old man had caused. The rest of the family seemed to have forgotten about it, but it was the one thing that Matt would never forget, and it was the one reason that he would never settle down and have a family of his own. The others hadn't seen what he had growing up; being the oldest by a couple of years had meant that he'd seen more of how their father had treated Mum.

Jake and Jenni's new house was spectacular—a long way from the old timber house where the McDougal siblings had grown up. The house where Matt now lived by himself. The two storeys had a sloping roof and wide shady verandas that wrapped around the four sides of the house which was painted in a soft grey. But despite its grandeur, it was a home. Comfy and colourful hammocks swung in the breeze on the first level, and Leni's trike and assorted toys covered the lawn. The house was welcoming, and Matt knew that their mother loved visiting here too. The last email had said how much she was missing them *all*, but Matt knew it was more the grandchildren that Mum missed.

Jenni's home oozed love and family, and when everyone was in the Bay, the family gathered here, but it wasn't often enough. Matt looked out to the Gulf and smiled. Three large vessels were moored close to shore. Jake's boat, *Moonshine,* was out there, and Donny and Dane and their partners had arrived by boat too. Matt quickened his pace, keen to see his family.

Laughter and voices reached him as he walked around to the large expanse of lawn at the back of the house. He smiled when he reached the outdoor kitchen that looked over the Gulf. He was relieved to see Jake had his arm looped around Jenni's shoulders, and Dane and Donny were leaning against the fence each with a beer in hand. There was no sign of Claire and Nicole, but he could hear voices coming from the kitchen.

The long table was covered with a colourful cloth, and he placed the bag he was carrying on the end.

'Hey, big brother.' He grinned as first Dane, and then Donny, enfolded him in a bear hug. Their father might not have been demonstrative, but Mum had ensured that the brothers were not shy about showing affection. Jake left Jenni and came over and thumped Matt's arm.

'Hi, big fella, I hear you've been busy.'

Matt nodded. 'And you too. Charters have been good so far by the look of things?'

'It's been a great start to the season. Lots of visitors in town.'

'Us too,' Donny said. 'I'm thinking about getting another boat. We've turned away heaps of bookings because we're full up. It's kept us busy, but now that Claire—' He broke off and grinned.

'And now that Claire?'

Donny shook his head. 'I'll wait until she comes outside.'

'The lodge is full too,' Dane said. 'We've had to hire more staff.'

Matt was pleased for them, but that glimmer of disquiet that had dogged him all week flared up again. He sat in the co-op day in, day out, while his brothers were out experiencing life. He pushed the thought away as Jenni took his arm.

'Did you get the coleslaw?'

Matt nodded and pointed to the chiller bag on the table. 'I got some fancy cheese and olives too. And there's a couple of bottles of wine in the bottom.'

Matt nodded as Jake held up a can of Coke. 'Yes please.'

'Thanks.' Jenni tipped her head to the side and tucked her hair behind her ear. Matt thought she looked tired. 'Did you go and see Maisie?'

'Yeah, briefly. She was holding court in the hospital foyer on a pair of crutches. Doc Rose was rolling his eyes. She was telling everyone about the new doctor and how pretty she is.'

'What new doctor?' Jenni shook her head. 'Of course, Maisie would know what's happening before anyone else in town.'

Matt hesitated. Of all his family, Jenni was the one who knew how badly he'd stuffed up with Sara. He should have been honest with her, but he'd known her so well she would have talked him around. That last night Sara had tried to talk to him, he'd been deliberately distant, and he knew he'd hurt her.

The next day she was gone, and he'd never heard from her again. Matt had been sad, but it had been for the best. He'd convinced himself that if Sara had really loved him like she'd always said, she wouldn't have left without saying goodbye, and she would have tried harder.

But that had been stupid. Even though it had been the outcome he'd wanted, he'd been bloody hurt, but the only one who'd ever guessed was Jenni.

If he'd had his time over again, he might have done things differently, but deep-down Matt knew it was for the best. It was what he'd wanted and how it had to be.

He looked up as his two sisters-in-law came out of the kitchen. Dane and Donny had hit the jackpot there, as had Jake with Jenni.

He hugged Claire first and smiled as she stepped back. 'You're looking exceptionally well.' He glanced across at Donny. 'Is there any news I should know?'

Claire's fair skin coloured but her smile was wide. 'Just that you're going to be an uncle again.'

Matt dropped a kiss on her cheek and then turned and shook Donny's hand. 'That's fabulous news.' Before he could turn back to greet Nicole, Dane held his hand out too. 'You might as well get it all over at once, Matt. Nicole and I have news too.' Dane's voice was husky as he smiled at his wife.

Nicole reached up and hugged Matt. 'Yep, another family member on the way here too. We called Binnie this afternoon, and now she wants to come back and live with her auntie and uncle.'

'Then you'd have your hands full.' When Nicole had first moved north, her small niece had lived with her in the old rundown house up the coast where they had now built their upmarket fishing lodge. Matt shook his head. 'Gawd, two more babies on the way. Mum will be beside herself. Rick won't get her away again for a while.'

'Yeah, we did a three-way Skype the other night. There was lots of champagne flowing on their cruise by the time we finished. They're going to extend the trip a bit, so Mum can have a couple of years at home. She won't leave the babies once they're born.'

Jenni sighed and pushed her hair back again. Matt frowned as he noticed her hand was shaking. 'Leni keeps asking when Nanny will be home. It's hard with her away with a new baby here.'

Dane and Donny went back to the barbeque to help Jake, and Matt turned to Jenni. 'You okay, Jen? You look tired.'

Her eyes welled as she looked at him. 'I'm just run down. Looking after the two kids, trying to keep the house in order, and I've had some sort of virus. I haven't felt well for a couple of weeks.'

'Have you been to see Doc Rose?'

She shook her head. 'No. I haven't had time.'

'Call me. I can come and sit with the kids.'

She waved a hand. 'I'm fine. I just need a good night's sleep. Jake's home for a few days now.'

Matt put his arm around her. 'You take care of yourself, sis.'

'I will. Now tell me how Maisie knows all about this new lady doctor we're getting?'

Matt swallowed and looked over the top of her head. 'Apparently, she ran into them in the Barossa Valley.'

'Them? We're getting more than one new doctor?'

'No. A friend of hers is coming with her.' He lowered his voice. 'Sara is coming home, Jen.'

Chapter Five

Next to the site Sara and Caro were allocated at Kulgera Roadhouse was a fire pit in an old truck rim. It was full of white ash and looked like it was well-used.

'What do you think?' Sara looked at the small pile of twigs beside it.

'I think a fire would be good.' Caro pointed across the narrow road behind the camp area. 'The girl on reception said there's plenty of wood in the bush if we wanted a fire. We have to collect it ourselves.'

'Let's go. We can set our swags up once we get the fire going.'

Sara and Caroline headed into the bush, keen to warm up. They'd both been surprised at how cold it was out in the desert. The days were warm and sunny, but the temperature plummeted to below zero during the night.

'Thank goodness we both have warm sleeping bags.' Sara shivered as they headed into the bush with a couple of bags to put the wood in. They didn't have to go far; there was plenty of fallen timber just behind the fence.

'You can tell you're from the tropics.' Caroline was still in a short-sleeved T-shirt and shorts.

'I never got used to the cold,' Sara replied. 'I'm so looking forward to getting back home.'

'You really have decided to stay there?' Caroline said as she bent to pick up a small dead branch.

'I have. Nan's getting on, and it'll be good if I'm around to help out when she needs it.'

'Did you tell her you're coming home?'

'No, I wanted to surprise her.'

Caro looked at her with a frown. 'Will you stay with her? If she's not expecting you?'

'I'll stay for a short while until I get my own place. I like living by myself.' Sara pointed to a dead tree on the ground at the side of the sandy track. 'And Nan'll be home. She never goes anywhere.'

'Do your parents live there?'

Sara shook her head. 'Gosh, no. Dad got out of the Bay when he went to uni and never went back. I lived with Nan from when I was fourteen when Dad got his first posting overseas. Dad's a diplomat and now he's at the embassy in France. They've been there for a few years. I don't think they'll come home even when he retires. They've bought a small cottage in a gorgeous little village called St Paul de Vence in the south of France. I'd love to go there

45

one day, but just for a visit. The photos Mum sends are gorgeous.'

'It's a very beautiful village.' Caro's voice was wistful. 'It's in Provence.'

'You've been there?'

'I have. I got engaged there.'

Sara paused as she went to pick up some kindling. 'Engaged? I didn't know you were— or had been married?'

'We didn't get married. Dylan proposed in Paris, and I said yes in St Paul de Vence a couple of days later.' Caro held out the bag for the kindling.

'You had to think about it?'

'You should know me by now, Sara, after working with me for a year. I don't rush into decisions. That's why I'll visit Second Chance Bay before I decide to take the contract. they've offered.'

'Fair enough.' Sara tried not to sound too curious, but she couldn't help asking. 'How long were you engaged?'

'Two years. I left him in Melbourne last year to come to Tanunda.'

'We make a good pair. What happened?'

As the two women broke branches off the dead tree, the top edge of a full moon appeared over the tree canopy to the east. They both stood there quietly as it rose until the heavy golden orb hovered over trees tinged purple by the sunset.

'I love the outback,' Sara said quietly. 'It makes everything else seem insignificant.'

'It does. To answer your question our situations were a bit different. Dylan didn't like that I was in a medical practice. He wanted me to go into research like he was.'

'He mustn't have known you very well. You are a fabulous practitioner. One of the best doctors I've ever worked with. You're patient, and compassionate and your patients all love you. Even the grumpy old men! That's why I'd love to see you take the contract at Second Chance Bay. Doctor Rose is a nice man and I'm sure you'd enjoy working with him.'

Caroline looked away and Sara caught the glint of a tear. Maybe it was best to change the subject.

'I think a full moon deserves a glass of Tanunda port around the fire. What do you think?'

'I agree.' Caro put the bag down and stared at the moon for a moment before she turned back to Sara. 'Thank you for being an ear, Sara. Leaving Dylan was one of the hardest things I've ever done. I loved him, and I thought he loved me.' She turned away again to look at the moon. 'A sight like that moon makes you believe in romance, but I learned the hard way. There is no heaver-after romance like in the movies. Not for some of us anyway. Dylan fell out of love with me. Once I told him I would be staying in practice, the last few months together were like living in an apartment with a stranger. We stopped doing things together, and he shut down. I stopped asking where he was when he was away all of the time. I never thought that he would cheat on me, and when he finally asked me to leave—'

'He told you there was someone else?'

'No. He told me he had simply stopped loving me, and that it was time for me to move out. He said it was because I wouldn't listen to him, that if I loved him, I'd do as he said. It was his apartment, so I had no choice.' Her eyes filled with tears and she brushed at them angrily. 'It toughened me up, Sara.'

'Oh, Caro, I'm sorry.'

'Even the last time he held me I still loved him, even though he'd broken my heart. He held me close and his lips brushed the top of my head, but I didn't cry. I packed my bag with my clothes, and I left everything else there, including the ring he'd bought me in Paris. I couldn't stand to stay any longer than I had to. It was awful.' Caro started walking and her movements were jerky as she bent and picked up small branches. She stopped and stared at Sara. 'You know what? I'm forty-five years old and I'm sick of being careful. I *will* take the contract at Second Chance Bay. What you've said about it being a good idea is enough for me. I'll email Dr Rose later.'

'Are you sure? That's fabulous!'

Although Sara was surprised at Caro's sudden mind change, she was happy. She could see Caroline living at the Bay, and Sara would do her best to help her find happiness.

'Now let's get this firewood and go back and have a wine to celebrate my new job.' Caro smiled and Sara felt as though their friendship had reached a new level.

'Sounds good to me.'

##

Once they had a cheery blaze going, Sara headed over to the amenities block for a shower while Caro sent the email accepting the contract. The amenities block was basic, but clean, and as she stood under the steaming hot water, Sara thought of ways to keep Caro at the Bay now that she had committed to the job. She was a fabulous doctor, and wonderful with all her patients—from small children to the elderly. She would be an asset to the community. She was sad for her; but determined to help her get over her broken heart.

When they arrived at the Bay, Sara had every intention of seeking Matthew out, so she could make it clear that they could be friends. She owed him an apology; leaving like she had, and never contacting him had been rude. An over-the-top kneejerk reaction. She knew she'd placed too much importance on getting married; she thought she'd loved him, but if she really had, could she have left like she did?

Yes, a small voice whispered. *You were hurt.*

No, logic chimed in. *You've managed your life very well without Matthew McDougal for the past few years. Rarely even thought about him.*

Rubbish, said that small voice. *You still think about him every day.* And that had been the problem with the relationship with Jeff. Maybe he had sensed that she wasn't totally committed to him, but he'd never said anything about that before he'd left her.

He'd left her.

Sara hadn't been as upset as she had been when she'd left Matt, but Jeff's rejection had made her realise that she had to learn to be happy spending her life alone.

And she *had* been happy at Tanunda. She'd got her head together enough to accept that it was time to go home to the Bay. Second Chance Bay where she had such happy memories.

Sara turned the shower off and reached for the towel. She was destined—and content—to spend her life alone. She could suit herself where she went and what she did. Maybe once she'd checked that Nan was okay, and got Caro settled at the Bay, she could go to France and visit Mum and Dad for a while.

If Matthew was still single, he might be an incentive to get Caro to settle there. She could be the right woman for him. A little bit older, but maybe . . .

Water droplets sprayed through the air as Sara shook her head with a laugh, but there was no mirth in it. She'd had success in setting up a few friends as couples since she'd left Second Chance Bay with her own broken heart. It was time to pull back.

Love and let live.

Woops, shouldn't that be live and let live?

By the time Sara had dressed and walked back to the campsite, Caro had put her laptop away and was sitting beside the fire.

'How about a real celebration?' she said. 'I checked out the roadhouse when I booked in, and the pub meals look okay. Let's eat inside tonight. My shout.'

'Sounds good to me,' Sara replied. The thought of cooking another meal and washing up camp dishes and pans in the cold air and red dirt didn't appeal.

They walked over to the log timber building and pushed open the door. The room was warm and inviting and to their surprise, they snagged the last available table near the fire. The room buzzed with conversation, and Sara looked around with interest. Older caravanning couples sat at the tables, and a few backpackers and a large group of ringers and cattle workers lined the long bar.

Sara grinned and pointed to the ceiling; a collection of Aussie flags, hats and baseball caps and different coloured bras hung from the slatted timber. 'Interesting collection.'

'Welcome to the outback.' Caro grinned. 'I've read about the collections in some of these roadhouse outposts. I'm looking forward to seeing the termite mounds that the backpackers dress up too.'

'You'll see them on the way to Second Chance Bay.' Sara looked up as a couple of guys stood at the side of the table.

'Do you mind if we share your table, ladies? Last seats left in the house?' A tall guy in a khaki work shirt stood beside the bench they were sitting on.

'Sure.'

As Sara and Caro moved along, a guitar chord reverberated through the room as the night's entertainer began to play; it was too loud to get into a conversation with the newcomers at the other end of the table, but the girls were far enough away from the speakers to still be able to chat.

'Different to the city,' Sara said.

Caro nodded. 'It is. It doesn't have that polished veneer that you see in city bars. This is a true snapshot of outback life.'

'I love it. A bit of a wild frontier feel. It's so Australian, it reminds me of home. There's a similar roadhouse on the back road on the way into Normanton too.' A huge wave of homesickness engulfed Sara. It had been a long time since she'd let herself think of the Bay, because the memories had made her sad for such a long time. Now the anticipation of returning to the town where she'd spent much of her life excited her. In a couple of weeks, she'd be home and would see Nan. It had been way too long; a twinge of guilt coursed through her. It had been ages since she'd called her grandmother for a chat.

'Tell me about the Bay.' Caro's grin was wide. 'I guess I should find out more about the place I've just committed to for a year. Dr Rose replied immediately, and he seemed pleased that I accepted the job. I guess I'll have to find somewhere to live when we get there.'

'That won't be a problem. There's quite a few empty houses,' Sara said. 'It's an aging population, or it was when I left. The younger ones move to the city, and sadly the elderly die.'

'That'd be right.' Caro pulled a face, but there was a smile there. 'Now I've accepted the contract you tell me the negatives! So, what are the positives?'

'Oh, the Bay is a beautiful part of the world. Wait until you see the Morning Glory cloud for the first time. The town is right on the Gulf of Carpentaria and there's a wonderful river full of birdlife and the odd crocodile if you like wildlife spotting. It's so interesting. I love wandering along the riverbank.'

'I'll pass on the crocs, I think.'

'The tourist industry is buzzing, and you can always get fresh fish and seafood.' Sara looked down. 'That's what Matt does. Or at least he did while I was there.'

'A fisherman?'

'No, he's an accountant. He looks after the books and the fish co-op for the family. It was Matt who told me we lived in an outback paradise. "Outback paradise right on the silvery sea", he used to say.'

'He sounds like a romantic?' Caro's glance was quick but curious.

Sara shrugged. 'I guess he was in some ways. I'll never forget the day we went out on his family's charter boat. As soon as we were out of sight of land, he was so seasick. His brother taught me how to fish, and I caught the biggest fish of the day.' The noise of the room faded as Sara looked at the fire and remembered that day. Matt had spent the trip in the cabin—and the toilet—but even though he'd known he would be seasick he'd wanted to take her out to sea. When they'd got back to the shore, he recovered almost immediately. Back then, she'd been in the spare room at Nan's house, and Nan had been away on a trip.

Matt had been pale, and she'd made him lie down on her bed. One thing had led to another and—'

'Which way are you heading?'

Sara jumped as the deep voice interrupted her daydream. The music had stopped, and the guy in the khaki work shirt had moved up the bench closer to her. His thigh pressed hard against her leg and she moved away.

'Oh, we've come up from South Australia and we're heading to Queensland,' she replied without being specific. They'd heard a few horror stories on the trip about some less than savoury characters in the outback. 'What about you?'

'We're not travelling at the moment. Me and my mates are helping with the mustering out at Avonlea

Downs for a couple of months. We're helicopter pilots and we do the circuit in the Territory.'

'Interesting.' Sara looked across at Caro and wondered if she was happy to be talking to the other guy. She appeared relaxed, so Sara settled back in her seat. It was funny, but she felt as though she needed to look out for Caroline, even though Sara was ten years younger than Caro.

The guy leaned closer and she caught a whiff of aftershave. 'How about I buy you a drink, lovely lady?'

She lifted her half-full glass of wine. 'I'm all good, thanks.'

With a shrug, he stood and headed to the bar and was soon talking to a couple of the backpackers that Sara had noticed earlier.

She closed her eyes and went back to her happy memories.

Chapter Six

Three weeks, four days, and three thousand kilometres after leaving Tanunda in South Australia, Caro and Sara drove into the small town of Normanton, an hour south of Second Chance Bay on the Gulf of Carpentaria. Sara knew that she'd been quiet since they'd turned north at Cloncurry onto the Burke Developmental Road. For some reason, her stomach had been in knots and the closer they got to the northern coast, the more it clenched.

'Slow down here.' She finally broke her long silence and Caro shot a swift glance in her direction.

'Are you car sick? You're awfully pale.'

'No, I'm fine. I was just going to point out . . . look. That's the croc I was telling you about.'

'Oh my God. It's *huge*.'

'"Krys the Croc" is a replica of the world's largest recorded crocodile. It was killed here more than fifty years ago.'

Caro shivered. 'And you've been telling me for the past month this is a good place to live and work?'

'Don't worry. It's safe. I've only seen a few crocodiles at the Bay.'

'Huh, only a few, hey? Thanks for the reassurance.' Caro flicked the indicator on and pulled over into a vacant car park. The red dust-covered vehicle barely drew a glance from the passers-by. 'According to my Nav Man, we're less than an hour away from your home. So how about a coffee and you can tell me what's been bothering you for the whole morning?'

'Sounds like a plan.' Sara unbuckled her seat belt and opened the door. 'Let's go look. I used to know where the coffee shops were in Normanton, but it's been a long time. My first job after I left TAFE was in the surgery here.'

They walked along the street and Sara watched the people she passed in the street. Normanton was the closest administrative centre to Second Chance Bay, and there was a good chance of running into someone she knew.

Not that they'd recognise her. She still had the curly auburn hair of her twenties, but these days it was a lot longer and she'd let the curls grow into spirals. In her time at the Bay, she'd lived in jeans and T-shirts and not the preferred primary coloured stripes that she favoured these days. She looked down with a grin at her purple tights, lime-green short skirt, and yellow and red striped T-shirt.

No, no-one would recognise *this* Sara Sweeney.

'Love it,' Caro exclaimed as she stopped at the front of a small shopping arcade.

Sara grinned as she looked at the sign outside the shop. The "Local Drips" coffee shop was an addition to the town since she'd left. 'Looks good to me.' She followed Caro inside and they sat at a table near the window.

A smartly dressed waitress was at the table within seconds, a pencil hovering above her order pad. 'What will it be, girls?' she asked.

'Lunch?' Caro raised her eyebrows at Sara.

'Sorry, it'll have to be something readymade from under the glass. We close in fifteen. It's Saturday.'

'Is it?' Sara and Caro looked at each other and laughed.

'Sorry, we've been on the road for weeks and lost track of the days.'

'Half your luck,' the waitress said.

Caro jumped up and went across to the refrigerated glass and called over to the table. 'A salad sandwich?'

Sara gave her the thumbs up. 'And a flat white for both of us, thanks,' she said to the waitress. As she waited for Caro to come back to the table, the door opened, and she looked up.

'Oh, my goodness!' Sara jumped to her feet and rushed across the room as Caro looked at her with a frown.

'Jumpin' Jehoshaphat, Sara Sweeney. As I live and breathe!'

Sara grabbed her grandmother's arms and then happy tears filled her eyes as she hugged her. She sniffed. 'What are you doing in Normanton, Nan?'

Her grandmother's face split in a wide grin, and she put a hand up to her neatly permed curls as Sara led her over to the table. 'What am *I* doing in Normanton? I think you'd better answer that one first, missy. What are *you* doing in Normanton? And more to the point without telling me!'

'I've come home, I wanted to surprise you.'

'Surprise me! You've given me a bloody heart attack.' Nan's face wrinkled as she frowned. 'And your timing is bloody awful, Sara. Why didn't you tell me you were coming? How long are you staying?'

'Why is it awful?' Before her grandmother could answer Caro came back to the table. 'Nan, this is my friend, Caro. She's going to be the new doctor with Doctor Rose. Caro, this is Nan.'

Nan reached out her hand to Caro. 'I heard there was a new doctor coming to town. Welcome.'

'Thank you. It's lovely to meet you. Would you like a tea or a coffee?'

'Please call me Ellen. A pot of Earl Grey would be good, thank you.' She stared at Sara and her frown deepened. 'Now tell me what's happening.'

Sara smiled. 'I've come home to stay, Nan. I'm going back to work at the medical practice as receptionist and the clinic nurse.'

'Well, that's wonderful to hear. I'm pleased you're here to stay and I won't miss you.'

'Miss me. Where are you going?'

'I'm going on a cruise to New Zealand with my cousin, Alma. I caught the morning bus down here, and I'm catching the two o'clock coach down to Cloncurry and then flying to Brissie from the Isa tomorrow.'

'Well, I'll be here when you come back.'

'Good. Where are you staying?' Nan pulled up a chair and sat down.

'Um, your place?' Sara tipped her head to the side and then frowned as Nan shook her head slowly.

'Sorry, love. You should have let me know.' She tapped her lip with one finger. 'You haven't changed, have you?'

'Sorry?'

'Never organised. All you had to do was make one call. I've got house sitters in for a month. I won't be back until next month. A sweet English couple are looking after Jed for me.'

'Jed? Who's Jed?' Sara was getting confused, and a little worried.

'Jed is my dog. He's a beauty. A rescue dog,' she said proudly.

'Oh well, no matter.' Sara waved a hand. 'I'll find somewhere to stay. There's always rentals.'

Nan shook her head. 'It might be harder than you think. Since they extended the zinc mine, and there are a lot more ships coming to the port, there's been an influx of workers. The rental market is tight in the Bay these days.'

'Oh.' Sara turned to Caro. 'I'm sorry. In my usual way—it sounds like I've given you some wrong information.'

'It's all right. Dr Rose said there's a flat at the back of the doctor's residence if I want it. You can stay there with me if you like until—'

Sara shook her head. 'It's too small. I know that flat. It's okay. I'll find somewhere.'

She ignored Nan's eye roll. Her self-esteem didn't need a battering.

##

Two hours later, Sara's complacency had all but disappeared. They'd seen Nan off on the coach and then driven to Second Chance Bay. As they'd driven past the sand flats and the wetlands on the southern side of town, the silver sheen of the Gulf glinted in the distance.

Caro had been quiet.

'Are you okay?' Sara had asked as Caro peered ahead at the narrow road into town.

'It's different to what I imagined.' Caro slowed the car as they entered the sixty zone. A faded sign hanging at an angle welcomed them to Second Chance Bay, and Sara looked around with fresh eyes. The town looked sad and neglected. As they passed the first residential streets, the yards were unkempt, and the grass long, growing high along the sides of the upturned fishing boats. A couple of old rusted utes sat on the side of the road—one with four flat tyres, and the other sitting up on bricks with no tyres at all.

'It's okay,' Sara said brightly. 'It's a shame that this is what you see when you drive in, but it gets better when we get over to Sunset Point.'

To her relief the residential area over at the point was still well maintained, and Caro had visibly relaxed as they'd pulled up outside the small medical centre. Unlike Sara, Caro was organised and had rung Dr Rose from Normanton. He had told her to come straight to the centre and he'd meet her there.

'Let's see if we can find room for you in the flat,' Caro said as they pulled up outside the old house.

Sara shook her head. 'No, honestly it's tiny, and you won't want me underfoot while you're settling in. It's okay. I've got friends in town'—she crossed her fingers behind her back— 'if you're happy for me to borrow the car while you meet Dr Rose, I'll get myself sorted and then drop it back. Is that okay?' She hid the tension that was building in her and smiled.

'Of course.'

As soon as they opened the gate, Dr Rose stood at the door and his smile was wide. To Sara's surprise, he hugged her in welcome and she stepped back to introduce Caro, feeling a little uncomfortable. Roger the Dodger had left a legacy, and she knew that was unfair because Hector Rose was a good man.

'I am delighted to meet you, Caroline.' He clasped Caro's hand and Sara smiled. She had never seen the doctor so animated, but to be fair it had been a long time.

Once the introductions were done, Sara left Caro at the surgery where Dr Rose was going to show her around the medical rooms and the flat, and she headed along to the point.

The sea was flat and silver and Sara wound down her window and took a deep breath. The salt smell and the sound of the birds wheeling above the boat ramp soothed her. Three small boats sat in the middle of the river and the horn of a large ship boomed a warning as it entered the river.

I'm home to stay, and I'll see this every day.

A reluctant grin tugged at her mouth. *Once I find myself somewhere to live.*

You're a ditz, Sara Sweeny, she thought.

But a ditz who'd come home. And was very happy to be here.

She'd just have to dig into her nest egg and pay for a room at the motel along from the caravan park. Parking the car, Sara took a deep breath and headed for the office on the other side of the road.

Chapter Seven

On Saturday afternoon as Matt was closing up the co-op, the phone rang. He hurried back into the office to answer it. Maisie had worked a couple of hours this morning—her injured ankle had healed—and it had given Matt a chance to catch up on the accounts. He looked up at the clock; he didn't fancy going home to an empty house. Maybe he'd go over to the pub for a quiet drink and a game of pool.

'McDougal's Fish Co-op,' he answered.

'Matt, it's me,' Jenni said. 'Have you got any plans tonight?'

'I was thinking about going to the pub.' Matt grinned. 'But it'll probably end up just the usual, a night at home by myself in front of the footie.'

'Half your luck. I'd give anything for a night of peace and quiet.'

'What's up, Jen? You need a babysitter?'

'No, we're having a barbeque. *Again.* Donny and Claire have been up at the lodge with Dane and Nicole this week, and they're all coming back to town tonight. Jake's invited them all for a barbie. I have to go shopping as soon as the kids wake up from their nap. And of course, they're both having an extra-long one today.'

Matt frowned; Jenni usually loved company, but she didn't sound impressed.

'So you come over too.'

'Okay. Where's Jake?'

'God knows. Probably down fiddling with one of the boats.' Her voice was short, and Matt thought she sounded as though she was on the verge of tears.

'Right. How can I help? How about I do the shopping?'

'Thank you. That'd be great. It's all right for Jake. All he has to do is light the damn barbeque.'

Now Matt was worried. In the five years that Jake and Jenni been together, he'd never once heard her criticise her husband, and that was the second time in one phone call.

'Leave it with me. I'll shop and don't you worry about any of the food.' Matt softened his voice. 'I'm worried about you, Jen. Go and have a lie down with the kids and have a rest.'

'I haven't got time. The place is a pig sty.'

'Jen. It's only us. Family. You know? We don't care what your place looks like.'

'Well, I do. I'll ring Jess at IGA and tell her I'll email an order through. All you'll have to do is pick it up.'

Matt gave up. 'All right. I'll have a shower here. I should have some clean jeans out the back. I'll be there in an hour or so. Okay?'

He frowned as the phone disconnected without Jen answering.

##

An hour later he pulled up outside Jenni and Jake's house at the northern end of the Bay. Callen, the baby, was screaming and every so often Matt could hear Leni's sobs between the screams. He quickly grabbed the pack of meat and the groceries that Jenni had ordered and hurried to the front door. When he rang the bell, Jenni yelled from upstairs.

'Come on up, Matt, I'm just getting the kids in their PJs.'

Walking across the wide expanse of glossy white tiles, he went into the kitchen and put the bags on the bench and the meat in the large double fridge in the butler's pantry before running lightly up the stairs.

'Everyone decent?' he called from the end of the hall.

'Yes. We're in Leni's room,' Jeni replied. The crying had stopped, and he walked tentatively to the bedroom, pleased to hear a loud giggle and then Jenni's soft voice crooning to the baby.

'Uncle Mattie, Uncle Mattie. Come and play dolls with me.' Leni stood at the door in her

68

pyjamas, her golden curls damp and clinging to her forehead. Jenni was in a chair by the window, breastfeeding Callen, their ten-month-old son. Matt smothered a grin. The baby wasn't wearing any clothes and Jenni pulled a face as she nursed him.

'The little monkey decided he was starving and couldn't even wait for me to get a nappy on him,' she said. 'He was screaming like a banshee.'

'I heard him. You're game to nurse him like that while he's feeding.' Matt chuckled. 'I'd hazard a guess? In one end and out the other?'

Jenni pulled a face. 'I've already been peed on . . . and worse today. Don't ask.'

'I won't. I couldn't do it. I'll stay an uncle, thanks. That's much easier, isn't it? How's the prettiest girl in the universe?' Matt bent down and picked up Leni. 'And my favourite girl.'

'She's very sad.' Leni's eyes were wide. 'Mummy didn't have time to dress my dolls with me. Callen was crying for his milk. Will you help me, Uncle Mattie?'

'Just for a minute because I'll have to go and get the barbeque going and the chairs put outside to help Mummy.' He glanced across to Jenni as he sat on the floor next to Leni. 'Heard from Jake?'

'Yes. Dane had a problem with one of the boats, so he'd gone up to meet them. They'll be a bit late getting here, so it gives me a chance to get the kids fed and in bed.' She smiled up at her big brother. 'Thanks for coming to help, Matt. I appreciate it. I'm sorry I was cross before.'

He waved one hand and took the Barbie doll that Leni passed him with the other. 'We all have good and bad days, Jen. I've been a bit down this week too.'

Jenni lifted Callen onto her shoulder and patted his back. 'What's wrong with you?'

Matt shrugged as he pulled the frilly dress onto the doll and handed it to his little niece. 'I don't know. A bit restless; the others are all doing interesting stuff, and I'm stuck in the office most of the time.' He forced a grin to his face to lighten the atmosphere. 'You know what I did today?'

'What?'

'I worked out how many times I've opened the door of the fridge.'

'Ooh.' Jenni shook her head. 'That's way sad, Matt. I think it might be time for a change.'

'That's where my thoughts were heading.'

Jenni crossed to the change table and tucked a nappy under her arm on the way. 'I get what you're saying, but you do know how much the boys appreciate what you do, don't you? All of them. You're indispensable to all the businesses, Matt.'

'I know. I guess it was—'

'Hearing that a certain lady was coming back to town?' Jenni's gaze was sharp. 'Be honest.'

Matt pulled a rueful face. 'I wouldn't admit it to anyone else, and don't you say anything, but yes, Sara coming back to town has thrown me a bit.'

Jenni walked to the door. '*I'll* throw her if she comes anywhere near me.'

Matt shook his head. 'No, don't you say a word.'

'Matt, I saw how upset you were when she left. And she never once had the courtesy to contact you or tell you why she did. And I'll talk to her if I want to.' Matt had spilled his guts to Jenni one night a few months after Sara had left. It was before she'd moved back to the Bay and had been teaching in Brisbane.

'Jen. Don't.' Matt's voice was firm and full of warning. 'Promise. Or I'm going home now, and you can do all of this by yourself. There's stuff between Sara and me you didn't know. Leave it.'

'Oh, all right. But I don't have to be friends with her.'

'No, you don't, but do remember I'm all grown up now. And you don't know what happened between us, but Sara going was for the best.' He pushed to his feet and ruffled his sister's hair as she walked past him with a sleepy baby in her arms.

'But I do appreciate the support. Come on, Leni. You can help me get the party ready.'

##

By the time the two boats were moored in the bay at the front of the house, the two little ones were in bed and asleep, Matt had marinated the steak, and the barbeque was alight. Jenni had made a salad and set the table, but Matt pushed her into the chair and poured her a wine when she said she had a load of washing to put on.

'Sit down, for goodness sake. It'll wait until tomorrow.'

'True.' She frowned when Matt passed her a glass of white wine. 'I haven't been drinking while I've been breastfeeding Callen. He might sleep extra well tonight if I have a drink.'

'One won't hurt, will it?'

'No.' Jenni shook her head. 'All good. And Matt, thanks for coming over. I really appreciate it.'

Voices and laughter reached them as Jake, and their two brothers and their partners walked along from the dock. Jenni lifted her face for a kiss when Jake came through the gate, and Matt was pleased to see the look of concern on her husband's face.

'I'm so sorry that I left you with all this, sweetheart. I'll stay home tomorrow and give you a hand.'

'It's okay, big brother Matt did it all. The only thing we haven't prepared is dessert.'

Claire smiled and lifted the Tupperware container she was carrying. 'The new boat has an incredible galley, and Nicole and I baked a dessert on the way down the coast. Lemon meringue cheesecake made with bush lemons from the lodge.'

'I found the recipe in this week's *New Idea*. I picked it up at the hairdresser,' Nicole said as she walked across to them.

'Yum, we're set then.' Matt crossed to the barbeque. 'You all go and have a wash and I'll get the meat cooking.'

'Okay, thanks mate.' Dane and Donny slapped him on the shoulder as they headed inside.

As Matt lifted the cover a sharp gust of wind blew in from the sea and caught the edge of the oval metal lid. It slammed down hard at an angle onto the hot barbeque plate and Matt jumped as pain sliced though his right hand.

Jenni jumped up and hurried over to where he stood grasping his fingers with his left hand. 'Let me see. Have you burned yourself?'

As Matt shook his head a wave of nausea washed over him. Blood was running down his wrist and dripping onto the path. 'Um, I'm pretty sure I've sliced the top of my finger off.' He looked down at the barbeque and had to close his eyes.

Jenni's scream was shrill. 'Jake! Come quick!'

Chapter Eight

Sara had been in luck. The hotel on the point near the small town's airport had one room left, and she booked it for two weeks. Paid the first week and hoped she might not have to stay here for the full time. She'd had enough motel stays in her travels to know what soulless places they were.

The girl on the desk looked at her curiously but didn't ask any questions. Sara recognised her; she'd been a couple of years ahead of her at school.

'We serve breakfast in the dining room from seven until ten, and if you want a night meal, you have to go across the road to the hotel.'

'Thanks.' Sara nodded and took the key that was being held out to her.

'Did you go to school here?' The woman's curiosity finally got the better of her. 'You look familiar.'

Sara nodded. 'I did. For a while.'

'Back on a holiday, hey? Not much of a place to visit these days.' The lips turned down into a dissatisfied pout.

'You think?'

A nod. 'What is there to do here for two weeks? Unless you like to fish?'

Sara grinned, although she was wondering why such a negative person was on the front desk of the only hotel in the Bay. 'I do, but I'll be too busy working to find time to fish. I'm starting work at Doc Rose's next week.'

'Oh wow, are you the new lady doctor we've all heard about? We didn't know it was someone local coming home.'

'No. not me. I'm the receptionist and nurse.' Sara leaned against the counter. 'But the new doctor is here too. We travelled up together.'

'Well, welcome home.' The girl, Jan, according to her name tag—her name had escaped Sara— leaned forward. 'I remember you. You went out with that sexy Matt McDougal for ages.'

Sara nodded without speaking and picked up her purse from the counter. 'Thank you. I'm pleased there was a room.'

The door squeaked as it closed behind her. She made her way to Room Sixteen and opened the door. The generic dull brown bedspread, the plastic jug and two white cups and saucers, and the obligatory packet of milk coffee biscuits faced her.

With a groan, she chastised herself once more for not ringing Nan to make sure she could stay there. Anyway, the couple of weeks–or maybe four—would go fast, and she'd keep herself busy at the surgery, and showing Caro the sights.

For the first time a little glimmer of doubt surfaced.

Was coming home to the Bay a backward step?

Sara mused as she drove back to the surgery. Even though she'd made friends in the towns she'd lived in when she'd studied for her nursing qualification, and worked in various medical practices, she'd never felt at home anywhere. The feeling that had overtaken her as they'd headed into the Bay earlier was enough to reassure her that this was where she wanted to be.

She grinned. Even if she had to stay in the old hotel for the first few weeks. It was her own fault; she should have told Nan she was coming home.

She looked at the Gulf as she drove Caro's car back to the surgery. The sea was a deep blue today as the wind blew in from the west. As she drove past the airport runway, a flock of Burdekin ducks waded in the sandy low tide shallows. Many species of migratory shorebirds came all the way from the northern hemisphere to breed in the wetlands and roosted all the way up the coast on the tidal mud and sand flats. Sara had spent many weekends birdwatching with Nan.

Contentment seeped through her; despite what Jan on reception had said, Sara knew she would have no problem filling her days at Second Chance Bay. She parked at the medical practice that fronted the small cottage hospital. As the permanent population of Second Chance Bay was less than five hundred, the hospital was more an extension of the medical practice. These days it was part of the North West Health Service area, but the locals had voted to keep the heritage name of Second Chance Bay Cottage Hospital. There was a wing with a small aged care facility, staffed twenty-four hours a day, but most patients were taken by ambulance into Normanton, where there were visiting specialist services. The closest major hospital was at Mt Isa over five hundred kilometres away.

Sara's job at the medical practice wouldn't be busy, but the work would be varied. She'd worked here before, so she knew what to expect. Sara had really enjoyed working with Caro in Tanunda, but she wondered what the doctor's impressions of the small facility would be. In one way, she was pleased that Caro had accepted the twelve-month contract before they had arrived, as the town—or the practice—might not meet her expectations.

She turned Caro's four-wheel drive—still covered with red dust— into the small car park at the side of the building, pleased to see that Dr Rose's vehicle was still there. She stepped from the vehicle and made her way to the side door where Dr

Rose had taken Caro. As she reached up to push the side door open, a white twin cab ute accelerated around the corner, engine roaring. Sara waited as it swung into the car park beside Caro's four-wheel drive.

Her heart skittered a tattoo of beats as the tall man stepped out. For a moment she'd thought it was Matt, but then she realised it was one of his younger brothers. He ran over to Sara, his face wrinkled in a frown.

'Is that Dr Rose's car? Is he here?' His voice was urgent.

'Yes, he's inside showing the new doctor around. Is there an emergency? Shall I get him?'

'No, I'll go. My brother is better off staying in the car until we know if they can help him here or not. He ran to the door, pushed it open and ran inside calling out. 'Doc Rose?'

Without hesitation, Sara hurried across to the car; she could assist until the doctor came out.

A blonde woman climbed out of the back seat of the vehicle.

'Sara?' she said with a frown. It was Jenni, Matt's little sister. Her face was pale, and she had dark shadows beneath her eyes.

'Hello, Jenni. Yes, it's me. What's wrong. Can I help?'

Jenni's voice shook. 'Matt has cut the top of his finger off. He's in the back with Donny. What should we do? Bring him in? Or take him to Normanton?'

Sara fought to control her reaction. Her heart pounded, and her mouth dried as she went across to the car. She recognised Don, Matt's brother sitting in the back seat. He was holding Matt's arm up high above his head.

Sara put her head in the open window. 'Good, keep it elevated, and if you can, get some pressure on the wound.' She swallowed as she looked across at Matt. 'Are you in much pain. Matt, or do you feel as though you're going to pass out?'

'I'm okay.' Steel-blue eyes held hers and her breath caught.

'Good. Do you have the rest of the finger?'

Donny nodded. 'Yes. It's packed on ice in a plastic bag. We weren't sure whether to come here or drive straight to Normanton.'

'*On* ice or *in* ice,' Sara asked with a frown

'No, it's not touching the ice. Thank God for Google.'

'Good.' Sara nodded. Her nerves were a jangled mess. Seeing Matt for the first time in so long and knowing he was hurt was surreal. 'You're in luck. You've got two doctors and at least one nurse here this afternoon.'

Jenni took her arm and pulled her aside. 'I Googled fingers as Dane drove. Matt's only got a limited amount of time before it's too late to save the finger.' She put a trembling hand to her mouth. 'He was so calm.'

'That's good and you're right, we have to be quick. But let's leave it to the medicos. Here comes Dr Rose now.'

Caro glanced at her as the two doctors hurried towards the car. 'Sara, there's no nurse on duty. Can you go in and prepare the surgery for a wound cleanse please?'

'I can.' Sara nodded and headed for the door. She tried to push away the thought of Matt being in pain. She knew that the doctors wouldn't give him anything until they'd assessed the wound.

By the time she'd found what she needed and prepared a tray in the small consulting room, the door opened. She was surprised to see Matt walk in, supported by a brother on each side. Caro and Dr Rose were close behind them.

'Thank you.' Dr Rose glanced at Dane and Donny. 'We'll examine Matt now while you wait in the waiting room. I think you need to keep an eye on Jenni; she looked as if she was about to faint. I'll get Sara to come out and check on her once we look at this finger.'

'I'll go out to the truck and get the ice bag,' Don said.

'Good.' Dr Rose nodded as the two men left the room.

'Sara?' Matt looked at her curiously. 'You're qualified now?'

She nodded. 'Yes. An RN.'

'Well done.'

The surge of pride that ran through Sara was incongruous with the situation. She glanced at Matt as Dr Rose helped him onto the bed. He seemed more interested in her being a nurse than he was in what the two doctors were doing.

Dr Rose and Caro went to the basin and sterilised their hands. Sara stepped back as Caro turned on the big light above the bed and Dr Rose unwrapped the bandage that someone had put on the wound. She took the chance to look at Matt.

Really look at him. Sara fought back the tumultuous feelings that churned in her stomach and sent butterflies running to every nerve ending in her body

Why did she feel like this? It was as though the eight years since she'd last seen him didn't exist. And that was *not* good.

She wasn't going to risk her heart again. It wasn't emotion or any leftover feelings; it was purely nostalgia with maybe some hormones thrown into the mix. Matt was still a very good-looking guy.

Sara turned away and busied herself at the surgical tray until the door opened and Don poked his head around. 'Here's the . . . here's Matt's—'

'Thank you,' she said briskly and placed the plastic bag on the tray. She wasn't squeamish usually, but she was unable to look.

'Perhaps you could go and check on Jenni now, nurse.' Dr Rose glanced at her. 'Are you feeling all right? You're a bit pale.'

'I'm fine. My red-headed complexion.' Sara forced a smile before she slipped out to the waiting room. Jenni jumped to her feet and put her hand to her head as she stumbled. Her two brothers caught her and helped her back to the chair.

'I'm sorry. It's all right. I'm okay.'

Sara didn't like her colour. Jenni was pale, but each cheek held a bright red rosy patch. 'I'll get you some water.'

'Thank you. Is Matt okay?'

Sara nodded. 'The doctors are with him now. You did well getting him here. How long ago did it happen?'

Dane shook his head. 'It'd be less than half an hour. We just put a pressure bandage on it and jumped in the car. We should ring the others and let them know the doctor was here.' He turned to Jenni by way of explanation. 'Jenni's husband is there with the two children and our partners stayed there too. I told them not to go anywhere near the barbeque. It was the wind blowing the lid that did the damage. I can't believe that it did so much damage.'

'Ah.' Sara nodded as she crouched in front of Jenni with a plastic tumbler of water. She was trying to process the changes in the McDougal family since she'd left.

'You're Sara Sweeney, aren't you?' the other brother, Donny, said. 'You used to come to our place with Matt.'

'Yes. I've moved back home to the Bay to work.'

'I thought I knew you. You've been gone a while,' he said.

Jenni lifted her head and stared at her, and there was something unknown in her eyes. 'Things have changed since you left.' She lifted her chin higher and her voice wasn't friendly. 'A lot.'

'I'm sure they have.' Sara put her hand on Jenni's forehead. 'You're running a temperature. I think you should see the doctor when they've sorted your brother.'

Jenni moved away. 'I'm all right. Matt's the one everyone should be worrying about. It's my fault.

He came over to help when I rang him. That stupid barbeque.''

'It was a freak accident, Jen. No one's at fault. We just have to wait and see if they think they can save it. And if there's time to get to wherever they would do it. Probably Mt Isa.'

'Or Brisbane,' Donny said.

For a moment Sara debated whether to say what she was thinking, and what she knew, but it wasn't her place to say. It was up to Caro and Dr Rose.

'If you're sure you're okay?' she said to Jenni.

The response was clipped. 'I'm fine.'

Sara turned away and opened the door of the examination room. The two doctors were at the end near the sink talking quietly and Matt was still lying on the bed, his eyes closed.

Dr Rose looked up and beckoned her over.

'We've given him a sedative. I know you're not officially on duty until the week after next, and I'd like to thank you for stepping in today. Are you feeling all right?''

'I'm fine.' She forced a smile; seeing Matt lying there injured was hard.

'What about Jenni?' he asked.

'She said she was fine, but I'm not sure. I didn't use a thermometer, but I think she could be running a temperature and she seemed unsteady on her feet.'

'I'll tell her to make an appointment to come and see me later. I have another request for you. Caroline and I have discussed it, and with Caroline's experience in microsurgery, we've decided to operate here. Matthew's chances of keeping his finger will be much better than the time it would take to fly him to Brisbane. There appears to be little damage to the bone and the tendons, and we have the equipment here to operate.'

'I'm happy to perform the reconstruction,' Caroline said. 'And Dr Rose will do the anaesthesia. It all depends on whether you're happy to assist, Sara?'

'Of course I am.' Sara didn't hesitate.

'Good.' Dr Rose said. 'Let's get started.'

Chapter Nine

The wave of pain drilled through Matt's fingers, up his wrist and into his shoulder. He clenched his teeth and fought it. He drifted off to sleep to blessed relief, and slept until a shadow fell across the bed. He opened his eyes and for a moment he thought he was dreaming.

It was like the recurring dreams he'd had for years. But now it was the real Sara standing there looking down at him with a strange look on her face.

'I'm pleased you came home to me, Sar,' he whispered. Her face faded and he drifted back off. When he woke next time, the new lady doctor was standing beside the bed.

She smiled down at him as she picked up the chart from the foot of the bed. 'Good morning, Matt. I'm pleased to see you awake. I'm Dr Morton.'

He nodded and gestured to the cup of ice at the side of the bed. 'Is it okay if I have some ice?' His voice was raspy.

'You can. You can even have some breakfast if you feel like it.' The doctor passed the small cup over to him.

'Where am I?'

'You're at Second Chance Bay in the hospital. We operated here.'

'I thought I'd dreamed it. So, it's all over and fixed?'

'It is.' She shook her head and relief flooded through him as she answered. 'You didn't dream it. You were very lucky that Sara and I arrived in town today. If you had to cut your finger off, you picked the best day for it.' Her laugh was musical and sweet, and it calmed him. 'Microsurgery was my speciality when I trained. Your injury was very clean, and it only took a couple of hours to get you sorted.'

'You've saved my finger then?'

'We're confident that it's going to be fine. Being your little finger meant there were less nerves to repair, but you're going to be in a bit of pain for the first day or two, and you must keep that hand elevated. But there's no reason why you can't go home tomorrow. Antibiotics will keep any infection at bay, and luckily you had a clean straight cut injury, your nerves may start to re-join in as little as three to seven days.'

Matt looked over as the door opened. He held his breath as Sara appeared in the doorway.

'Is it okay if I come in?' she asked.

Matt nodded. 'Yes.'

Sara walked over to the bed and stood next to the doctor. 'Hello, Matt,' she said softly. 'How are you feeling?'

'I'm good.' He nodded again. 'Welcome home. I hear you're home to stay.'

She shook her head. 'I haven't decided yet. Just for a visit at this stage.' He didn't miss the curious look the doctor shot Sara's way.

'Anyway,' Sara said. 'I came to make sure you'd met Caro.'

'Caro?' He frowned.

'Me. I'm Caro,' the doctor said. 'And Sara's friend. We've just done a road trip right up the centre together to get here.'

'Ah, the Thelma and Louise.'

Sara's nose wrinkled into that cute button-shape that he'd seen many times before. A tug of nostalgia took away the ache in his hand briefly.

'Thelma and Louise?' she asked.

'Maisie told me it was a movie. You should have told me you were coming home, Sar.'

'I should have.' This time her smile was rueful. 'And I should have told Nan I was coming home too, and then I wouldn't be staying at the hotel.'

'Plenty of room at the McDougal house these days,' Matt said.

Jeez. Matt couldn't believe he'd said that.

'Oh, I wasn't angling for an invitation, Matt. Nan's got someone staying at her place while she's away. The hotel is just a temporary measure.'

'The offer is there.'

Bloody hell. Next thing he'd be proposing.

Sara looked at him with a smile and it seemed forced. 'Thank you. Look, I'm sorry we lost touch, Matt. I *was* going to come over and see you.' She gestured to his bandaged hand. 'Before this happened, anyway.'

'I'll leave you two to catch up. I'll call in a bit later, Matt.' Caro nodded and walked to the door.

It was clear Sara didn't want to stay. Matt gestured to the chair at the side of the bed and her eyes widened like those of a rabbit caught in the headlights.

'Sit down. We've got a lot of catching up to do.'

She hesitated and then sat stiffly in the plastic chair. 'Come on, Sar, we can be friends. Lots of water under the bridge in what? How many years?'

'I forget. Probably seven or eight.'

He held her gaze as she lifted her head and her eyes were bright.

'We can be friends,' she said. 'I'd like that. That's why I was going to come and see you—to clear the air. It's too small a town to have any awkwardness. I guess we'll be running into each other most days.'

'We will.' He kept his voice soft. 'It's been a long time since you left—' Matt bit off the "me" just in time. 'And I was surprised when you left so suddenly, but it was for the best for you.'

'It was.' She nodded and looked down at her hands folded in her lap.

'This town was too small for you. And you wouldn't have been able to do your nursing if you'd stayed here. You've achieved a lot, Sar.'

Neither of them mentioned the conversation they'd had that last night. Matt wondered why it was so easy to remember every word eight years later.

'Tell me about the Bay, Matt. About your life. I see the rest of your family are settled with partners and kids. You?'

There was no way he was going to tell Sara that even though he wouldn't settle into a relationship the few times he'd been on a date, he couldn't get past the memory of Sara, and he'd given up going out.

'Me?' Matt winced as he shrugged, and the pain shot down to his fingers. 'You know me. Too busy working for there to be time for anything else.'

She nodded but she was quiet.

'The business has expanded, and it keeps me busy. I'm there by myself most days. Maisie's just come back for the winter and she'd been doing some hours for me.'

'Will she work for you while you're off?' As Sara leaned forward a spiral of red curls fell over her face and she pushed it away. He remembered running his fingers through those tangled curls.

Matt's mouth dried as Sara stared at him. 'Could you pass the water, please?' he managed to choke out.

He sipped through the straw, and the iced water eased the ache that had suddenly lodged in his throat. 'I won't be taking any time off. I can operate a computer and type into a spreadsheet one-handed. The doc said I can go home tomorrow.'

'Fair enough.' She stood. 'I should go and let you get some rest.'

Matt held out his good hand and took hers before she could move away. 'What about you, Sara. Is there a significant other in your life?'

She hesitated for a moment and then nodded. 'Yes, I met Jeff about four years ago.' She tugged her hand away. 'I really must go. I have things to do. Take care, Matt.'

Chapter Ten

Sara was out of breath by the time she'd walked back to the hotel.

Truth to tell, she had nothing to do. It had been too hard sitting one-on-one with Matt, and she'd had to get away.

Sitting there beside him as he'd lain on the bed; his strong profile turned to her, she had realised how foolish it had been to come back. Her feelings for Matt hadn't changed one bit. She'd had to clench her hands in her lap. The need to reach out and gently brush the hair back from his face had been overwhelming.

Coming home was very different to what she'd imagined it would be.

She went to bed early and tossed and turned in the hard bed all night.

##

'Hi Sara. Come in. I've just boiled the kettle.'

Sara pushed open the door of the small flat at the back of the medical surgery. She wrinkled her nose. 'Have you been baking already, Caro? Or is that delicious smell wafting over from the hospital?'

'I did some shopping and I felt like cooking. So there's a raspberry and coconut slice almost ready to come out of the oven.' Caro bent down and opened the oven door a little bit. 'Yep, almost done.'

'Yum. Count me in.' Sara pulled out the stool at the kitchen bench and looked around. She knew this apartment well; she'd often used the kitchen when she'd worked as a receptionist in the practice before she'd moved away. 'You've settled in okay by the look of things.'

Caro had flair and the small kitchen bore the evidence of her homemaking skills already.

'I have. I'm so pleased that you told me about Second Chance Bay. I've had a lovely welcome. Dr Rose is a sweetie, and I love the cottage hospital.'

Sara bit back a smile. A sweetie was the last term she'd use for Dr Rose. He was a serious man who rarely smiled. 'And you haven't even seen the medical practice in operation yet.'

'No. I'm looking forward to that next week.'

'Have you got everything you need here, or do we need a trip down to Normanton?'

'I'm pretty right. I went for a walk around to the IGA yesterday afternoon and got the basics. It's a friendly town; I had quite a few chats on the way home.'

'It's not every day the town gets a new doctor. You'll be welcomed with open arms.'

Caro nodded. 'And it's not every day you get to operate in the hospital the same day you arrive in town.'

'True. Matt was very lucky we arrived yesterday. It's such a long way to the next big hospital he probably would have lost the top of his finger.'

Caro smiled. 'On the way back from the town centre I called into the hospital to see him. Matt McDougal seems to be a very nice guy too.' The glance she shot towards Sara was curious.

Sara nodded and she knew her voice was hesitant. 'Yes, Matt is a good guy. But don't go getting any ideas, Caro. He's not the man for me. We had had a good talk and cleared the air. We decided we can be friends.'

'Are you sure?'

'Yes, I am. I've been there. Been there, done that.'

'Got the T-shirt.' Caro's dry comment made Sara smile. She already seemed happier than she had been at Tanunda.

'I could have. It's time to get on with life. I'm home where I wanted to be. We've ironed out any awkwardness and it's all good.'

'If you're sure. So if you have had a talk and you're going to be friends'— again that curious look—'you'll be fine about going around and dressing his finger at his place when he goes home?'

'Not a problem.'

'It's healing well and I'm happy to send him home later today on the condition that he gets his finger dressed. He can't do it himself of course. Matt said that his brothers are heading back home now that they know he's okay and Jenni is busy with her children.'

'Of course. It's also part of my brief as clinic nurse. So just tell me what you want me to do there and how often.'

'Okay, I will. We'll leave it bandaged for the first few days, but I'll send the dressing kits and the saline solution home with him when he leaves. I'll get you to check on him once a day. Just to watch for infection and temperature.'

Sara nodded as the timer on the oven rang. 'Morning tea time.'

Caro picked up an oven mitt, opened the oven door and slid out the slice tray. As she placed it on the wooden board to cool, she glanced at Sara. 'Speaking of Jenni, I'm going to try to see her this week. Do you think she'll make an appointment to see me or Dr Rose? She certainly didn't look well.'

'She's not happy with me. I picked that up loud and clear. But that's understandable. I guess the family think badly of me for leaving Matt. From what Matt he said he was pretty peed off, but, hey, that's the way the cookie crumbles.'

'You're very blasé about it, Sara.'

'Caro, it was eight years ago. A lot's happened since then. I've had one serious relationship. I've had different jobs and lived in some interesting places. I've got my qualifications. You can't go back to the past.'

'I guess you're right,' Caro said as she brought the kettle back to the boil.

This time it was Sara who looked at Caro curiously. 'You know, Matt McDougal might not be a bad way for you to fill in your year in town.'

'You just leave me alone, Sara Sweeney. I don't need anyone organising my social life or my love life. The kettle's boiled. Do you want tea or coffee?

Sara looked at her thoughtfully as she poured the water into the teapot. If Matt took Caro out, it would take any attention off her. She'd feel more at ease, Jenni might stop being so cross, and the locals wouldn't wonder what was happening between her and Matt.

Yes. Sara nodded to herself as Caro pulled out two white mugs. It was time to pull out her matchmaking skills.

#

Sara walked to the hospital mid-afternoon. Caro was already there meeting with Dr Rose and Sara glanced at the four-wheel drive they'd spent the last month in. She smiled; Caro had been busy; as well as baking and making herself at home in the flat, and looking after a patient, she'd still found time to clean the car. The paintwork was gleaming and only if you looked very closely could you see a trace of red dust in the wheel hubs. The interior of the car was empty and the swags and camping gear had been stored somewhere.

Sara pulled a face. While Caro had been energetic, what had she been doing? Walking around town feeling sorry for herself.

Second Chance Bay hadn't changed much in the years she'd been gone. The streets between the Gulf and the small shopping centre were bare of grass since the dry season had arrived. Grey sand added to the depressing vista of houses with faded paint and sagging guttering. She walked past Nan's house, and was pleased to see that the grass was mowed and the garden was tidy.

She pushed open the door of the clinic and the smell of freshly-brewed coffee wafted out. Dr Rose had always been a coffee connoisseur and it would be a bit better than the coffee that had been delivered to her room this morning. The sachets of

Black & Gold coffee on a tray with a pot of lukewarm water didn't quite make it.

Sara knew she had to get herself set up; there was no reason why she couldn't go and shop. No reason apart from being organised, and that's what she'd always found hard to do. Caro was already organised, and had her apartment sorted; she should take a leaf out of her book.

Maybe when she got settled at Nan's, she could get her thoughts together a bit better, although living there would be a temporary measure. She frowned as she walked into the office at the back of reception. There was no reason why she couldn't find a place to live now. She'd go and see the council office today. The Bay was too small to have a real estate agent. Or it used to be—maybe she could ask Matt.

If the truth be known, she'd spent too much time thinking about Matt McDougal for the past twenty-four hours. It was only the worry of what he'd done to his hand, she rationalised. Nothing more.

And if you believe that, you're off with the pixies.

'It's only that I haven't seen him for a long time,' she muttered. 'And I'm worried about him.' Sara jumped as Caro walked into the room.

'Who are you talking to?' she asked looking around

'Um. No one.'

'Matt is right to go home this morning.'

'Is he getting picked up?'

'No, he said he's right to take himself. I questioned that, but he assures me he doesn't have far to go.'

Sara put her hands on her hips. 'He mightn't have far to go, but did he tell you he has to go home by boat?'

Caro screwed up her nose. 'By boat?'

'Yes, Matt lives on the other side of the river and there's no bridge.

'Okay, I'd better make sure the dressing has a plastic cover to make it waterproof.'

'It's not only that. He's not going to be able to start the runabout one-handed.' Sara sighed. 'I'll take him home.'

'Are you right to do that, Sara? Do you know what to do? What sort of boat?'

'It's an aluminium runabout. Or it used to be. There's probably a new one these days. I've been over to the other side of the river many times. I haven't forgotten how to start Matt's boat. Or if he's got a new one, it won't be hard to figure out.'

'You're certainly full of surprises, Sara.' Caro shook her head and then said briskly. 'Okay. He's right to go. Hector and I have already seen him.'

Sara smothered a grin at the "Hector". She'd never heard Dr Rose referred to by his Christian name by any of the locums before.

They walked together from the surgery into the small cottage hospital.

Caro smiled. 'I already love this place. It's going to suit me very well.'

Sara nodded. 'It's only early days yet. You might find it boring after a while.'

'I'm sure I won't. Hector was telling me how busy it's been since the mine expanded. New families in town, and the days are always busy.'

'Different to when I was here before,' Sara said. 'Nan said there were new people in town.'

Matt was sitting on the side of the bed fully dressed as the two women walked into the small ward. He was the only patient in the small hospital.

'So, I hear you're going home today.' Sara avoided his eye and looked at the wall above his head.

'Yes, this morning, according to both the docs. I'm just waiting for the all clear.'

Caro nodded. 'You're right to go. Sara will be coming to your place to change the dressing every day for the first few days.'

Matt nodded slowly. 'Can't I do it myself?'

'Not one-handed. And I'd be more comfortable for Sara to check it every day. Infection at this stage could compromise the healing.'

Matt didn't look too impressed as he stood. His hand was elevated and strapped in a sling against his shoulder. 'Fair enough.'

Caro left them and Sara leaned against the doorframe with her arms folded. 'So you're ready to go?'

'Yes.'

'And how do you intend doing that?'

Matt lifted his chin and held her gaze. 'The same way I have for the past thirty plus years.'

She huffed a sigh. 'I'll take you. Have you got any gear to take?'

'I'm fine, Sara.'

'I don't think so. How are you going to start the boat? You seem to have forgotten very quickly that you've just had half your pinkie finger sewn back on, Matt.' She stared at him and a ripple of nostalgia ran through her as he held her gaze steadily. 'I'm taking you. It's already sorted with Caro. Unless one of your family is coming to take you over?'

'No. And I'm quite capable of getting myself home.'

'I'm sure you are. But while you're under my watch, I'll take you.'

'Not yet.' Matt grunted as he walked to the door. 'I was going to go to the co-op for a while.'

'What?' Sara stared at him in disbelief. 'In the fish co-op? What for"

'Working in the shop.'

'Serving food?' Sara stared at him

He nodded stubbornly. 'Someone has to do it.'

'Well, Matt. That someone isn't going to be you. For several reasons. Risk of infection to you. And hygiene. You'll have to call someone in or close the shop.'

Matt went to fold his arms and winced as his arm brushed the bandaged hand against his shoulder. Frustration rose from his gut and he tried not to get cross. He and Sara were standing in the small garden at the front of the medical clinic.

'Bloody stupid accident,' he muttered digging into his jeans pocket for his phone. 'Excuse me for a moment.' This time Matt's temper rose as he tried to hold the phone and put his password in at the same time.

One-handed.

He flicked a glance at Sara as she cleared her throat. 'And you thought you could go to work? And then drive the boat?'

'Don't be a nag. Can you put—' He broke off as he remembered.

'Can I put what?'

'Can you put my password into my phone please, and then dial Maisie. She's in the contacts. Under M.'

'Sure.' Sara held her hand out and he passed her the phone. 'What's your password?'

'260884.' Heat warmed his neck and he lifted his chin. 'I never changed it. Couldn't see the point in remembering a new one.'

Sara typed the numbers—her birth date— into the locked screen without commenting. Knowing that her birthday was Matt's password was strange. She didn't know what to think about that. A few seconds later, she passed the phone back and he held it to his ear.

'Maisie? Hi, it's Matt.'

'Hello. What's up?' Her gravelly voice sounded as though he'd woken her up and Matt glanced at the time.

'I was hoping you'd be able to work today.'

'It's Sunday.'

'Yeah, I'm sorry, but I've had a bit of an accident and I can't get there.'

'Bloody Nora. You must be half-dead if you're not going in. What's wrong? You *never* miss a day's work!'

'Long story, Maisie. But I'm okay. Just a problem with my hand. Can you work? Even just a couple of hours to freeze yesterday's fresh prawns.'

'I'm sorry, Matt, I can't. I'm down in the 'Curry for the day. There's a poker tournament at the bowling club.'

'No matter. I'll sort something. Have a good day, and good luck.'

'Thanks, love. I'll be back late tonight, and I'll come and give you a hand tomorrow.'

Matt disconnected the call with his thumb. He was going to have to call Jenni. She hated working in the co-op and hadn't worked there since before Leni was born. He handed the phone to Sara again. 'Sorry, Sar. I feel so bloody useless. Can you dial Jenni, please? She's in contacts under JJ.'

Sara took the phone back and obliged.

It didn't pick up for a few rings and Matt was waiting for voicemail to kick in when Jake finally answered.

He sounded short of breath. 'Hey Matt, how are you today?'

'I'm on my way home, or about to be. Is Jenni handy?'

'Sorry, she's still in bed. She had a bad night with Callen, and I'm minding the kids this morning. She woke up with a headache so I've sent her back to bed. I'm going to take the kids out for the day and give her a bit of a break. Can I help?'

'No, it's okay. What about Dane and Donny and the girls? Have they left yet?'

'Yeah, they went at first light. They said to tell you to get better quick.'

'Thanks.' Matt went to scratch his head and the sling tugged. 'Tell Jen I'll catch up with her tomorrow. Have a good day with the terrors.'

'Bye, mate. And listen I'm bloody sorry about your finger. I've chucked that lid out. I didn't realise it was dangerous.'

'It was just an accident. I'm on the mend. I'll see you through the week, Jake.'

'See ya, mate.'

Matt put the phone down and took a deep breath. 'Sar? I'm really sorry but I need a big favour. A really big favour.'

Her smile was tentative as she looked across at him. 'Okay, shoot.'

'If you come over to the co-op with me, I promise I'll sit away from the counter and any seafood.' As he watched he saw the faint trace of a blush on her cheeks. 'I won't go anywhere near the product. I need you–'

'You need me to freeze down yesterday's prawns?'

106

He nodded sheepishly. 'Um, yes and the fish. We had a big delivery yesterday, and the day was quiet.' He rushed on as she stared at him. 'I'll owe you big time. I know you don't like the touch and the fishy smell.'

'It's okay.' She looked away and her voice was cool. 'I've done it before. I think I can remember what to do.'

'I'll take you out for a meal to say thank you.'

She shook her head. 'There's no need for that. A favour between friends. Come on. It'll be a yucky job but the sooner I get it done, the sooner I can get you home and you can lie down. You've just had surgery, Matt. You need to take care of yourself.'

'Okay. I'll do whatever you say. And thank you.'

'Are you right to walk across to the co-op or do you want me to go back and get a wheelchair?'

'Bloody hell, Sar. It was only my finger. I'm not crippled.'

Chapter Eleven

Sara deliberately walked slowly as they crossed the road at the corner up from the hospital. The fish co-op was only one block from the medical rooms and hospital, but she didn't want Matt to overdo it. It was less than twenty-four hours since he'd had a general anaesthetic.

'I guess I'd better think about getting a car if I'm going to stay up here,' she said before she thought.

'Is your partner going to move up here?'

Sara groaned inwardly. How was she going to get out of this one?

'Um, yes. Eventually. Probably.'

Matt glanced at her as she walked along beside him. 'What does he do? What did you say his name was?'

'Um, Jeff. He's in finance.'

'Not a lot of call for that up here.'

Sara thought quickly this time. 'He's an investment banker in Melbourne. He'll probably retire before he comes up. So, it will be a while before that happens.'

'What? When he's sixty?'

'No, um sooner than that.'

'And he's going to come with a view to staying here without even seeing the place first? It's not exactly got the Melbourne coffee shop scene I'm sure he's used to. How old is he anyway?'

'About your age.' Sara crossed her fingers behind her back. The chances of Jeff ever meeting Matt were zero so she could embellish the truth a little. He was actually a couple of years younger than she was and that had been much of the problem.

'Ah, for a while I thought you'd found yourself a sugar daddy.'

Sara refrained from stamping her foot on the paved path that ran along the front of the hospital. 'Come on. Let's get this done and we can get you home. I have other things to do.' She strode ahead towards the corner near the river.

Truth was, she didn't have anything to do. Until she found a place of her own or Gran came home, she was stuck in a bit of a no-man's land. The hotel room was not actually a place where she wanted to spend her day.

She could go start looking for somewhere to live. That would fill in the rest of the week until she began her job at the practice.

Matt caught up to her and walked along quietly beside her; the silence was a little bit uncomfortable.

Sara swallowed. It wasn't his fault. She was the one who'd come home, and it was up to her to make it work. They'd already decided they could be friends, but the tension in her had been caused by the conversation about Jeff. That had been stupid. She sighed as they reached the co-op.

'Don't worry, it won't take long. I was thinking as long as you do the prawns for me, I can give the fish away to the charter company for burley.' Matt reached into his pocket and pulled out a set of keys.

Sara shook her head as she opened the door for him. 'Sorry. It's not that. I'm happy to help, and I'll do whatever needs doing. I was just thinking about finding somewhere to live. Who looks after the rentals here now? Is it still the council office?'

'No, that closed a few years back. The council operates out of Normanton now.'

'I guess I need to go down there to buy a car anyway. Two birds with the one stone and all that.' Sara stepped in as Matt held the door open with his good hand. 'Thank you.'

'The mine does it now. There's an office over in the old town. They do the rentals for the new families that move in. I'm sure if they had anything, they'd let you look at it. But there's not a lot available at the moment.'

'Yeah. Gran said there were a lot of new families arriving in the Bay.'

'The mine's been good for the whole town. Even our businesses. The young blokes are cashed up and they take our shorter charters out to the Gulf on their days off.'

'That's good to hear.'

'It is, but there was a lot of resistance at first to the mine expansion from the older residents. But they can see now what good it's done for the town.' Matt nodded as he lifted a stool from behind the counter and put it over near the door. 'Is this far enough away to be hygienic?' His grin tugged at Sara's heart. Talking to him was like old times, but in those days, he would have held her hand as they'd walked. She swallowed.

Leave it.

Her voice was businesslike. 'It is. You sit there and tell me what to do.'

Matt leaned against the wall and obliged. 'In the fridge on the back wall, there are two large bags of fresh prawns that were delivered fresh yesterday. They came in on the trawler about midday so they're still fresh enough to freeze down.' He pointed to a large double-door fridge cabinet beside the window. 'And there's a roll of large freezer bags on the cupboard next to it.'

Sara nodded as she lifted out the roll of bags. 'Okay. I've got them.'

'Bring them over to the counter, and then bring one bag of prawns over at a time.'

Sara opened the fridge and the salty smell of fresh seafood met her. It wasn't *too* bad. The fridge was neatly arranged, and the contents of each shelf were labelled. The two bags of prawns were on the bottom shelf in a large blue tub. She picked up one bag and carried it over to the counter while Matt watched.

'Tip a good lot on the scales and get it as close to a kilogram as you can.'

'I'll have a wash before I start. Same bathroom?'

He nodded.

Sara walked towards the office and pushed open the door to the bathroom. Nothing had changed; the room was clean and tidy with a blue towel hanging next to the wash basin. She quickly washed and dried her hands and walked back to the shop area. Matt was looking out the window at a car that had pulled up. He pulled a face.

'Customers. They saw me through the window as they drove past. I'll put the closed sign on the door. I don't usually worry about it as we're open most of the time.'

'No. Leave it. I'm happy to serve if you tell me what to do. Silly to turn away business.'

'Thanks, Sara. I really appreciate it. I feel so bloody useless. My little finger, for goodness sake! Who'd have thought that could incapacitate a bloke!'

'It'll be healed before you know it.' She put on a stern face.' As long as you do as you're told and look after it.'

'Yes, Sister Sweeney.' Again, that grin made her tummy all squirmy.

The bell above the door tinkled and a young couple came in with a small boy.

Sara stood behind the counter. 'Morning,' she said brightly.

'Hello.' The man stepped up to the counter. 'I was after some bait. We're taking our son fishing.'

Sara glanced over at Matt. 'Bait?'

He went to stand, and she shook her head. 'Uh uh. You tell me.'

'The freezer cabinet next to the door,' he said as he turned to the guy at the counter. 'What sort of gear have you got? And are you going out in a boat or from the shore?'

The guy laughed. 'This is our first time. We bought a plastic reel and hand line at the IGA store, and when we went down to the river, we realised we needed something to put on the end.'

'To catch the fish,' the boy said.

113

'We've just moved here,' the young woman said, 'and we have no idea what we're doing. We're from Brisbane and Danny has started work at the mine.'

'Okay.' Matt nodded. 'A bag of small prawns will do the trick, Sar. Top shelf, left basket.'

She found them and carried them to the counter.

'Watch out for your dress, there's an apron folded on the shelf underneath the register. Sara reached down and slipped the yellow plastic apron over her head as the man walked over to Matt with the little boy. The woman stood at the counter and pulled out her purse.

'I'm just filling in for today,' Sara said. 'I've just moved to town too.'

She wrapped the prawns and noticed a price list stuck to the side of the register. 'That will be six dollars-fifty.' The woman handed over the right cash and Sara put it on the front of the till before she wrapped the frozen prawns in the white paper that was beneath the counter.

'Where are you from?' the young woman asked.

'Originally from here, but I've been away for a long time. Matt hurt his hand and I'm helping him out.' She grinned and caught Matt's eyes as she looked across the room.

'You're doing well, Sar. I might hire you.' His eyes were alight with humour.

'Sorry, I've already got a job.'

'Where do you work?' The woman held out her hand. 'Sorry, I'm Marcy. We haven't met anyone yet. We've only just arrived this week and Danny started work the next day.'

Sara took her hand and shook it. 'Hi. I'm Sara and that's Matt.'

Matt nodded at them both and lifted his sling. 'Sorry I can't shake hands, but good to meet you.'

'And this is Justin,' Danny said.

'Hello, Justin. How old are you?' Matt asked.

'I'm six and I go to big school now,' Justin replied. The two men started a conversation as Sara handed the bait over to Marcy.

'Where do you work, Sara?' Marcy asked again.

'Sorry. I start at the medical clinic next week.'

The young woman looked shy. 'You're the first person I've met so far. Maybe . . .maybe you'd like to have a coffee one day? Or maybe we could all have lunch one weekend?'

'Oh. Matt and I aren't—'

Matt looked up. 'We'd love to have lunch with you both one weekend. Sara has just moved back to town and we're getting reacquainted.'

Heat ran up Sara's neck. Things were moving a bit fast, although the "getting reacquainted" that Matt talked about was certainly not the way her imagination had been going. She would have to put a brake on her thoughts.

'That'd be great,' Danny said. 'That was my only worry with bringing the family up here. It's such an isolated area and most of the workers at the mine are single guys.'

'We both grew up here, and it was okay, wasn't it, Sar?'

She nodded. 'It's a great place to live. I've come back home for good.'

Marcy looked curiously from Sara to Matt. 'I'm going to try and get some work while Justin is at school, but I know it will be hard in such a small place. If you hear of anything, I'd appreciate it.'

Matt caught Sara's eyes and smiled at her.

Damn butterflies. They were tromping around her stomach now.

'I know where there's a job going,' he said.

Marcy's eyes widened. 'You do?'

'It might not be what you wanted, but the hours will fit. What did you do before?'

'I was in retail. I worked in an electrical appliance store in a suburb in outer Brisbane. I was on the counter, but my main job was doing the accounts. I have references.'

'When can you start?' Matt asked with a grin.

'What here? In the fish shop?' Marcy's eyes were huge now as she turned to her husband.

'If you're happy to work with seafood.'

'Oh wow, yes. Oh, Matt, thanks so much. What a day it's turned out to be. I can start as soon as you want me. Justin goes to school tomorrow, so I'll have to take him and get him settled in the morning and then I'm free until three o'clock.

'Perfect. I'll see you after you drop him off.'

Sara cleared her throat. 'Perhaps Maisie could show Marcy what to do.'

Matt chuckled. 'I didn't think of that. It might get confusing.'

Marcy frowned. 'Confusing? Is it still okay?'

This time the chuckle turned into a laugh as Matt stood and crossed to the counter. 'I meant having a Maisie and a Marcy working on the roster.'

Marcy put her hand to her chest and let out a relieved sigh and then she smiled. 'Not to mention Matt!'

Matt held out his left hand and squeezed Marcy's. 'I'll see you here in the morning and yes, I'll get Maisie to show you the ropes. I can spend the day in the office. Is that okay, Sister Sara?'

'I guess it is.' Sara couldn't help the smile she gave him. 'As long as you rest today.'

Matt rolled his eyes at her and returned the smile.

117

The butterflies started their clodhopping again and Sara knew she was in trouble.

Chapter Twelve

Their boat trip across to the small residential section on the west of the river was uneventful. The aluminium runabout dingy was the same one the family had used when Matt used to take her across when they'd been seeing each other.

'How's your Mum?' Sara asked. 'You've never moved out of home?'

'No, *I* haven't.' Matt chuckled as she steered the boat across the river. 'But Mum moved out. I'm the only one who lives there now. Pretty boring, hey? A man of my age still living in the house where he grew up.'

'Not boring at all. It's a lovely old place, and I know how much you loved living here on the river.'

Sara glanced down at Matt when he didn't reply. She was standing at the back of the boat holding the tiller. It was a lovely morning and the river was flowing sluggishly. On the far bank away from the houses, she could see a pair of jabirus standing in the mud flats. The sun was glinting on the shallows, and as she watched one of the birds leaned forward putting its bill into the water and stood motionless waiting for the opportunity of snaring a fish.

Matt's voice was quiet, and Sara had to lean forward to hear him over the sound of the motor. 'I've been thinking of that a bit lately.'

'And?'

'I think it's time for a change. The others have all got their businesses set up and going well. They're based here and away. Jenni's busy with the kids and Jake has a great business going. Did you know when he left here after school, he went to the French Riviera?'

'No, I didn't.'

'And Dane and Donny have their businesses, so I've been feeling a bit—'

'A bit what?'

'Staid and stagnant, I guess. I'm thinking about moving. Trying something new.' Matt stood as the boat approached the shore. 'If you pass me that rope, I can throw it on the post one-handed.'

Sara picked up the rope, leaned forward and passed it to him. Her fingers brushed his and she turned back to the motor, ignoring the little thrill that ran up her arm. Matt's words about moving away were some she would have to remember. He hadn't been prepared to settle down with her eight years ago—she hadn't been what he wanted—and now it looked like he was going to leave town. If he did move away it would make her life a bit easier— emotionally, that was.

He threw the rope to the post and snagged it perfectly. Sara cut the engine and the boat rocked slightly on the wash that followed them in. She sat on the wooden seat in the middle and waited for it to stop.

'Stay there. I'll get out first and then give you a hand to get out. The last thing you want is to fall on your hand. It would undo everything Caro did,' she said.

Aware of his proximity, she held her dress close to her legs as she stepped up to the wooden jetty that was at the back of the McDougal house. Holding out her hand Sara braced herself for Matt's touch, and as soon as he was safely on the jetty, she let go.

Stupid butterflies in her tummy.

'Caro seems like a nice woman,' Matt said as they walked together towards the back gate. 'Have you known her long?'

'She's a lovely person and a fine doctor.' Sara was pleased to hear that Matt was impressed with Caro. It was one step in the direction of getting them out on a date. 'We've worked together in in the Barossa Valley for the past twelve months. I was at the practice when she arrived, and we hit it off straight away. I really enjoyed travelling up here with her.'

Matt stepped to the side so she could open the gate to the garden at the back of the house. Sara held it open for him, but he stopped and looked at her.

'You worked in the Barossa Valley? Isn't that in South Australia?'

'Yes, why?'

'I thought you said your partner was in finance in Melbourne. I assumed that's where you lived. That's where you moved to when you left here, wasn't it?'

Sara nodded and closed her eyes as she walked through the gate. How the hell was she going to explain that?

'Yes, it was. How did you know that?'

'Your grandmother told me.'

'Oh.'

Matt walked next to her and all was quiet as he waited for her answer.

Finally, he stopped at the back door. 'I'm sorry. I'm probably being too nosy.'

Sara simply shrugged. It was too hard to answer without telling more lies, so she changed the subject. 'I've lived in a few places. Where are you thinking about moving to?'

This time Matt shrugged. 'Hard to say. I've got to give it a bit more thought. But it's good to have someone listen to my whining. I haven't mentioned it to anyone else.'

'My pleasure. It's hard to know what you want sometimes. I've been there. I'm happy to be your sounding board.'

As they stood at the door, Matt reached over and took her hand with his uninjured hand. He held it as they stood there, and Sara looked at the ground.

'Thanks for seeing me home, and thanks heaps for wrapping up all those prawns. I got Dan's number and it would be nice to welcome them to town. What do you think about going to the pub for lunch one day next weekend if it suits them?'

'Sounds like a plan. I'll invite Caro too. Then they'll know someone else in town.'

'Excellent. I'll give Dan a call.'

She nodded and pulled her hand away. 'You take care of yourself. Go and have a lie-down, and don't do anything. Have you got something for dinner tonight?'

A strange look crossed Matt's face and he shook his head. 'No, but I can open a tin of something.'

'You most certainly will not! I'll bring something over later. I have to take the boat back to get home, so it leaves you stranded. I didn't think of that. Not that you could drive it anyway.'

123

'True. I guess I'm dependent on you.' Again, the look on Matt's face was strange and Sara wondered if wanted her to come back or not.

'I'll get a hamburger and drop it over, but I won't stay,' she said.

'If you're sure it's no trouble?'

'This week is fine because I'm not at work. You should be right by next week.' Sara turned away. 'I'll come back at six. Promise you'll rest?'

'I promise.'

As she went to walk back to the boat, he called out to her. 'Sara?'

She turned slowly. Matt was still at the door watching her and Sara smoothed her hands over her dress nervously.

'Yes?'

'Thank you for looking out for me. And thank you for listening.'

And that made her feel even worse about lying to him. She lifted her hand in a brief wave, before she hurried back to the boat.

**

Matt stood at the door until the sound of the motor died, and the boat was moored safely across the other side of the river. As Sara got out of the boat and tied it to the wharf she didn't turn around.

Her yellow dress clung to her thighs as the wind whipped up and he stifled a groan.

What the hell was he going to do?

One look at Sara Sweeney, one afternoon in her company, and the feelings he'd held for her came rushing back.

No, they hadn't come rushing back, he reminded himself. They'd never left him. He'd just learned to push them away as he'd tried to forget about her.

But her return was timely.

He'd been thinking about going, and now he would. Staying away from Sara was necessary. She was the one person who had come close to breaching his determination never to marry.

Matt closed the door and walked to his bedroom. He lay carefully on the bed with the sling holding his injured hand firmly to his chest. He closed his eyes and tipped his head back.

He loved Sara Sweeney. He always had and he always would.

Matt knew he had to remember his vow. He had a temper like his father had—but he had managed to keep it under control as he got older. But it still simmered beneath.

With a deep breath, he cast his mind back to his teens. He was the oldest of the four McDougals, and he wondered sometimes if he was the only one who remembered what their father had been like.

A gambling and abusive drunk.

He knew that Jake hadn't liked Dad, and that he had caused the fracture in Jenni and Jake's relationship that had seen Jake leave town.

Dane and Donny had spent a lot of time at sea on the other boat to Dad, and he wondered if that was how they had stayed out of his range. But Matt had been the one in the fish co-op and the office during his teens and his early twenties before Dad had died. He remembered one time that Dane had threatened to take Dad out the back and deal with him. Dad had come home drunk and given Mum a mouthful and thrown his dinner on the floor.

'What's this shit, woman? A man'd be better off having a feed of prawns at work instead of coming home to this mush.'

But their father had laughed at Dane and gone to bed and passed out.

Like he did most nights.

Mum had blossomed after Dad had died. She was happy.

Matt knew he was the one who carried the scars of his childhood—both physically and emotionally. He knew that he'd been the only one who'd copped a flogging when he was little; Dad had stopped when Matt grew tall and filled out. The one time he'd gone to hit Dane, Matt had been about twelve and he'd stepped in. But Matt still had the scars to show what he'd grown up with.

No one—not even their mother—talked about their father these days, and there were no photos of him in the house.

And that says it all, Matt thought.

The next time he was tempted to touch, kiss, think about, or even be in Sara's company, he'd remember the scar on his stomach, the one where Dad had kicked him and broken his rib because Matt had forgotten to lock the door at the co-op one Saturday evening.

When he and Dad had arrived on the Sunday morning to an unlocked door, his father had been suffering from too many beers the night before. He had pushed Matt over and then kicked him while he was down.

'Don't you ever forget to lock that door again,' he'd bellowed.

Matt had managed to work all morning to keep the peace, and it was only later that night when he was having trouble breathing that Mum had taken him to the hospital. He'd told the doctor back then that he'd tripped and fallen on the corner of his bed. Mum's expression had been full of anguish, but she'd stayed with Dad.

No. He shook his head as he lay there.

He would never take the risk of being like his father. It was safer to be alone. It was bad enough that he looked like him, and he was terrified that he'd inherited that gene for drinking and gambling.

And violence.

Sara Sweeney was safe. It was good that she had a partner. Another reason to stay away from her.

Matt lay there and vowed that he would get over Sara. He knew how close he'd come to succumbing the night eight years ago when she had hinted that she wanted to marry him. He had been so close to taking her in his arms and saying that's what he had wanted too.

But he'd managed not to, and the next morning she'd left town.

And he vowed that he would leave the Bay at the end of the year. It would give him six months to find an accountant who could take over, tell the family it was his time to follow his dreams, and think about where he wanted to go.

The problem was he had no idea where he'd go or what he'd do.

Matt lifted his arm and put the back of his hand over his eyes and tried to sleep.

Chapter Thirteen

Sara left the boat at the back of the McDougal's fish co-op and hurried back to the medical practice to see Caro. She knocked on the door of the flat, but there was no one there. With a frown, she went to the door of the medical practice, but it was closed and locked; there were obviously no patients for the afternoon's surgery with Dr Rose. There was no one at the hospital so she went back out to the street and stood undecided. She had nowhere to go until she went back across river later with Matt's hamburger.

Even that in itself proved problematic. So far, her return to Second Chance Bay had been very different to what she'd expected. No grandmother home, nowhere to live and then Matt McDougal and his accident.

It would be rude to run in with his dinner, and then leave, even though she'd said that was what she would do. He'd probably need a hand to cut it up, and then wash up afterwards. As much as she didn't want to go back to Matt's, she knew she would take her dinner too, and stay there for a while.

Matt McDougal terrified her. Not once in the two years that she'd been going out with Jeff—

they'd never lived together—had she experienced that yearning that she did when she was in Matt's company. The need to look into his eyes, the desire to reach up and touch his face, to caress his hair, or to simply lean against him.

The simple act of being with Matt made her happy. A different type of happiness than any other she'd experienced in her life.

A unique emotion: a feeling of completion and anticipation at the same time.

The memory of that simple physical relationship made her feel sad. No longer could she freely touch him or put her arms around him. The desire to touch him when they'd been at his house had made her fingers ache and tingle.

The memory of being with him, when they'd slept together, was one that she pushed right away. There was no going back to those heady and happy days.

The thought of Matt leaving the Bay filled Sara with confusion. If he left, she wouldn't have to deal with him making her feel like this, but the thought of him going away and not seeing him upset her. It was as though the past eight years hadn't happened; she felt exactly the same way she had when she'd been here.

Whoa, girl, hold your horses. Nan's voice was so clear in her head, it was like she was out on the street with her.

Sara shook her head as she thought about how upset she'd been the night Matt had rejected her. And Nan had been upset too, and had encouraged her to get away.

'But I didn't think you'd go away for so long,' Nan had said when the first year had passed.

Focus on that and forget all this squishy tummy, lovey-dovey feeling.

It was lust, pure and simple. Matt was a good-looking guy. She hadn't been on a date, let alone had sex for well over a year. She and Matt had been very compatible—in *all* ways—and that's why she'd thought there was a future for them.

For Matt, it had obviously been sex and nothing more. He'd never considered a future together.

So why was she letting herself get so taken with him again?

Because you're a fool, she thought.

Sara straightened her shoulders and set off for the small business district in the centre of the original township of Second Chance Bay. From this moment on, she was going to stop fluffing around. She was going to stop daydreaming about Matt McDougal and a totally imaginary future.

He hadn't wanted her before, and neither had Jeff.

No one had. She'd tried not to let it bother her, but her parents had even left her when she was only fourteen. There'd never been any mention of her moving to Europe, and luckily Nan had wanted her.

About the only person who ever had.

Sara had hidden her pain behind a bright and ditzy exterior for a long time.

And she was tired of pretending. She was going to go and find somewhere to live and make a future for herself. A happy future, here in her home town.

And when she bought Matt's hamburger, she'd drop it off and then go straight home.

There was no need for manners. He could wash up when his hand was better.

The new Sara had been born.

Half an hour later Sara's mood had lifted. Even though it was Sunday, the mine office had been open.

'We have to be here, in case of emergency,' the admin officer explained. There were two rentals immediately available; both on this side of the river, and both with reasonable rent.

'If you're keen, you'll have to put an application in today, Sara, because they'll be snapped up. It's really unusual for us to have any empty houses, let alone two at once. Normally we wouldn't consider someone who doesn't work at the mine, but as you are a health professional and will be providing a service to our workers—indirectly—I'm happy to let you apply.' The administration officer gave her the addresses and two keys on the proviso she would return them within an hour. 'The second house is actually for sale, so I can only give three months lease at a time on that one.'

'That's fine for me to start with.'

Sara set off full of enthusiasm and she didn't think of Matt for a full hour.

Well, maybe half an hour, but it was a start.

The first house near the shopping centre was too big for one person, so she headed off to the second house. As soon as she walked into the street, she knew which house it was going to be. She'd walked past the gorgeous little cottage every day when she'd gone to high school. It was ten years since she'd left, and Mrs Plummer had been elderly then.

According to the mine guy, the elderly woman had gone to an aged care facility in Normanton close to where her two children now lived.

Sara stood outside the house and smiled. It was *exactly* as she remembered it. The gardens were full of colour, flowers nodded along the inside of the front fence and the lawn was green. Huge trees ran down each side inside the fence line providing shade for the gardens that ran beneath the windows. The house was an old Queenslander with a central staircase that ran up to the front door. The windows were still covered by the lace curtains she remembered from high school.

Sara ran quickly up the front steps and put the key in the door. It opened with a creak and the sweet smell of lavender greeted her. Even though she'd loved the house as a teenager, she'd never been inside and she wasn't disappointed with what she saw.

The carpet was a soft grey with a burgundy rose pattern. There were a few pieces of furniture left in the house, enough for the essentials. The bathroom had the original 1950s basin on a pedestal in a deep pink, with a matching bathtub. The kitchen was quaint, and the house was high enough to see the river and catch the breeze.

Sara stood at the window and looked to the west. If she stood on her toes, she could see the McDougal house.

Enough. Stop it, she chastised herself.

One more quick walk around, with a brief stop at the overflowing bookcase in the living room, and she locked the door and hurried back to the office.

'I'll take it,' she said as she handed over the keys.

'Which one?'

'The smaller one. The house on Rosedale Street.'

'Excellent.' He found the required paperwork, and Sara pulled out her Visa card, and within ten minutes she had leased a house for three months.

'If I have anyone wanting to look through it for purchase, I will always give you at least two days' notice.'

'That's fine,' Sara said. 'I'll be at work in the daytime, and I'm not a messy person.' She turned to leave, and a thought struck her. 'How much is the house?'

The figure that he named was less than half of what she expected, and Sara was thoughtful as she walked out of the office.

It would be manageable, and the price was so low, it would barely mean a loan. Sara had saved hard over the past few years, always knowing that one day she would need to purchase a house of her own.

She left with the key clutched tightly in her hand, keen to get to the motel and check out. She'd only paid a week upfront and was happy to forgo that to get out of the boxy motel room. The rest of her things were in Caro's shed, and she wondered where Caro was this afternoon.

Sara walked back through the small shopping mall and was about to cross the road when she spied

Caro through the window of the only coffee shop in town. She changed direction and across to the café. As she opened the door, Dr Rose walked out and Sara was taken aback when he gave her a dazzling smile. She ordered a cappuccino at the counter before she made her way to the table where Caro was sitting with papers spread out in front of her.

'Feel like some company?' she asked.

Caro looked up with a start. 'Sure, grab a seat, just let me clear this away.'

'What are you doing?'

'Just filling in all the forms for the medical practice and the hospital. I've signed the contract, and this is all the other stuff. Honestly, it gets worse every year. It was easier to do it when Hector gave it to me, rather than take it back home.'

'Weren't you at the hospital?'

'Yes, but he had the paperwork at his place, so we came here for a coffee and went through it.'

'Sounds like you're getting on well.'

'Yes, he's going to be a good boss, and he's really pleased to have another doctor on board. He just got called over the wharf. You know since the mine expanded, he's been on call seven days and nights a week!'

'He will be pleased to have you here then.' Sara looked up as the waitress brought her coffee over. 'Thank you.'

Caro looked at her curiously. 'You said Hector was here when you were here before?'

'Yes, he's been here for about twenty years.'

'Oh. Does he have a family here?' Caro toyed with the spoon on her saucer.

'He was a bachelor when I left here. I haven't heard of any change. Why?'

'Just curious. He works very hard.'

Sara smiled. Maybe there was a new incentive to keep Caro in town.

'How did you go with Matt? You didn't overturn the boat or anything?' Caro shook her head. 'I can't believe you took him home in a boat. How on earth did you manage that?'

'It was like riding a bike. It all came back.'

'How was he feeling?'

'He's okay, but I think I'll have to watch him. He thought he could work at the store on the way home, but I sorted him out.'

Caro laughed as Sara told her about selling the bait and wrapping the prawns. 'There's no doubt about you, Sara. You can lend yourself to any situation.'

'Oh, and we met a new couple in town, and Matt organised a dinner at the pub. He said to bring you along too.' Sara crossed her fingers behind her back.

'Nice. I'm really settling in. It feels as though we've been here a week not a day and a bit!'

'I know, and I've found myself somewhere to live already.' Sara picked up her coffee. 'And you know what? As crazy as it sounds—'

'Crazy?' Caro grinned. 'Sara Sweeney doings something crazy? Never!'

'Don't be mean. Anyway, as I was saying before I was rudely interrupted, I think I'm going to buy the house.'

'Buy it? Are you that sure you're going to stay in town?'

'I think so.'

'Buying a house is a big step for only "think so".'

'Okay, I know so. I'm home. I'm settled. Matt and I have sorted out the past, and we're going to be friends.'

Caro looked at Sara over the top of her glasses and didn't say anything for a moment. 'Okay. I guess you know your heart. But be wise.'

##

A few hours later Sara called in at the pub and as she stood waiting for her order to be taken, her thoughts buzzed to and fro.

Will I get one or two?

It was early and there were only a few people out in the beer garden that would fill up as the sun set. It was an iconic spot for taking sunset photos and Sara and Nan had often come down to watch the spectacular colours when she'd lived here.

She was still considering her options when the waitress came to the counter.

'What can I get you, love? Eat in or takeaway?'

'Takeaway please.' She swallowed and came to a decision. 'Two hamburgers. One with the works and one plain, and a large chips please.'

'Be about ten minutes.' She took Sara's money and handed her a slip with a number.

Sara walked out onto the grass and sat at one of the wooden tables beneath the big tree. The muted noise coming from the pub faded. It was quiet outside and only the noise of the small boats returning from a day of fishing broke the silence.

She took a deep breath of the fresh salty air and looked out over the silver water of the Gulf. She loved this town, and she loved being near the water.

And she adored that little house, and she didn't want anyone else to live in it.

If she bought it, it would be a good reason to stay in town. Nan wasn't getting any younger, and she would love to have her only grandchild close by. Before she could change her mind, she pulled the mine agent's card from her purse. She dialled his number on her phone and it picked up immediately.

'Hello. Mr Ryan? It's Sara Sweeney here.'

'Hello, Sara. Everything okay with the house?'

'Yes. Very okay. I wanted to make an offer on it.'

'Oh. That's good.'

Sara offered a figure ten thousand below the asking price.

'I'll get onto the vendors and get back to you by tomorrow.'

'Thank you.' Sara smiled as she disconnected and hoped that the offer would be accepted.

As she walked along the riverbank towards Matt's boat, she shook her head, but her smile was wide.

What the hell have I done?

Chapter Fourteen

Matt dozed on and off all afternoon. Sara filled his thoughts when he was awake, and when he slept. The sleeping dreams were more explicit than his waking thoughts and brought back memories of the six months that they had been together. It was hard to let go of that sweet feeling of contentment as he lay there staring at the ceiling.

The light was fading when he woke for the third time. His mouth was dry, and his head and arm were aching. When he stood, the room spun, and Matt grabbed for the table next to the bed. He sat on the edge of the bed until his head stopped twirling, and then made his way slowly and carefully down the hall to the kitchen.

Pulling out a chair he moved it one-handed to where he could see the back gate. It wasn't long before the sound of the boat's motor drifted across the water and in through the open window. Sadness filled him as Sara appeared at the gate and walked slowly along the path to the back door.

He loved her so much it was almost impossible to bear. He put his hand to his head and covered his eyes as the last of the afternoon light seared into his brain. That was why his eyes were wet. Angrily he brushed the back of his hand across his eyes and by the time she pushed the back door open, he had regained his composure.

'Matt,' she called quietly as she stood at the porch inside the back door. 'Are you awake?'

'I'm in the kitchen, Sara.'

No more Sar. It was too intimate.

Sara stepped into the kitchen and took one look at him before throwing the plastic bag on to the bench. She hurried across to the table and put her hand on his forehead.

'You have a temperature.'

'I feel like crap.' His voice was croaky.

'Have you taken anything?' Her hand was cool on his forehead.

'No, I just woke up and came into the kitchen.' Matt was disappointed when Sara moved her hand away.

'I'll get you some paracetamol to bring the temp down. Any other symptoms?'

'A headache and a bit dizzy when I got up.'

'Any pain in your hand?'

'No more than there was.'

'That's good.' She rummaged in the bag that was hanging on her shoulder and pulled out a slide of tablets. 'We'll get your temp down and I'll call Caro.'

'No need for that.' Matt shook his head. 'I'm fine. I must be. I'm hungry. I can smell hot chips.'

'And we both know your weakness for hot chips,'

Their eyes met and held, and an uncontrollable surge of need ran through Matt. He reached up and took Sara's hand and slowly pulled her close. He leaned his head against her stomach and closed his eyes. She stood beside him and didn't move. Her unique perfume surrounded him, and the warmth of her body soothed him. After a moment, she lifted her hand and softly caressed his hair. The contentment and yearning that flooded through him were stronger than ever.

'I'm sorry, Sar.' His voice was husky, and his throat ached. 'I'm so sorry.'

'What for, Matt?' Her voice was a whisper.

He shook his head. 'I'm just sorry.'

She seemed to understand because she stayed there with her hand on his hair for a long time.

***

The grief in Matt's voice was clear. Sara knew that he was apologising for what had happened before she'd left town, but she didn't know how to respond. It wasn't fair to push him while he was

143

unwell, but a tiny glimmer of hope flared in her chest as they stood there.

Eventually she lowered her hand and moved away. He lifted his head and stared at her and she was taken aback to see the moisture clouding his beautiful blue eyes.

'I'll get you a couple of tablets.'

He nodded and the strange moment was broken. She turned her back and walked to the sink, sensing that he needed to compose himself. She automatically opened the cupboard where the glasses were kept and pulled out two glasses. After filling both at the sink, she crossed back to him and placed one glass in front of him and handed him two painkillers.

As Sara crossed back to the sink, she worried about Matt. He was obviously feeling unwell to show his vulnerability—she knew it had always been there— but he'd always been the strongest, oldest sibling. He'd run the business, she'd seen him care for his mother when their father had died suddenly, and he'd looked out for the family.

She picked up the glass of water and drained it and then reached for two plates. When she turned back to the table, he was watching her carefully and she smiled.

'Do you feel a bit better now?'

'I do.'

She lifted out the larger burger and placed it on the plate. She looked around for the knife block that had been on the bench in the days she had spent many meal times here, but it was gone.

'Where's the knife block?' she asked.

'Mum took it with her when she moved in with Rick.

'Rick?'

'Mum's partner. Or fiancé, I should say. They're in Europe at the moment.'

'I'm pleased your mother has found a new partner.'

'She's very happy.' He pointed to the drawer beneath the window. 'There's a sharp knife in there.'

Sara opened the drawer and picked up a serrated knife She carefully cut the large burger into four pieces and managed to keep it all together.

'Don't forget my chips,' Matt said with a cheeky grin.

'Who said they were for you?' she replied.

Matt's eyes were brighter now, and the dull flush on his cheeks had faded. She tipped a good serve of the chips onto his plate, and then sat down.

'What about you?' he asked. 'Where's yours?'

Sara picked up the bag and took out the smaller burger and put it on the plate. 'I'm not really hungry. I had coffee and cake at the shops with

Caro not that long ago. Oh, and I told her about dinner at the pub and she was keen.' She stared down at the plate. The main reason she had invited Caro to dinner was to push Matt and Caro together. But now she wasn't so sure.

Matt had confused her. His determination to leave town, and his strange apology a minute ago; she didn't know where she stood with him.

'Your chips are getting cold.'

Sara picked one up and chewed it to keep him happy.

'What are you thinking about, Sara?' he asked.

Sara forced a smile to her face and looked at him. 'I was wondering if I over-shopped today.'

'Is it possible to over-shop in Second Chance Bay? Last I heard the last dress and shoe shop closed a few months back.'

Sara picked up another chip and looked at it thoughtfully. 'No, I *really* shopped. I think I bought a house.'

Matt put the second quarter of his burger down and stared at her.

'A house? Why would you do that?'

'Because I'm going to stay here.' A frisson of nerves jerked through her body and Sara swallowed.

In for a penny and in for a pound.

Matt had been honest with her. This skirting around the truth wasn't the best way to move back to town. He'd been clear that they could be friends, and friends were honest with each other.

It was time.

Sara put the uneaten chip back on her plate. 'I'm going to be honest with you, Matt. You've been upfront with me.' When she looked at him, he looked over her head and a muscle jerked in his jaw. 'I've been a little bit loose with the truth.'

She sat up straight and this time he met her gaze.

'Jeff and I split up before I moved to Tanunda. I just didn't want you to think I came back here to try to pick up where we left off.'

He nodded and spoke slowly, but it was impossible to read his expression. 'I see.'

'I've decided to stay here. I've got a great job. Nan needs me and I love the Bay. I'm here to stay. When I saw Mrs Plummer's house was for sale, I couldn't resist.'

Again, the nod. 'I'm really pleased for you, Sara.'

No more, no less. No, "I'm really pleased you're staying."

Matt picked up the next piece of his burger and his focus was on that. Disappointment shimmied through Sara.

But really, what had she expected? Did she think Matt would declare his undying love, and fall to his knee and propose?

She bit back the sigh that threatened to rise.

Of course, he wouldn't. He didn't love her, and he'd simply needed comforting before. He was unwell.

'Do you have a digital thermometer here?' she asked.

Matt shook his head. 'No.'

'How do you feel now?'

This time he smiled. 'Better. My headache has gone, and I don't feel as doughy. All I needed was chips.'

That sexy smile sent a shaft of longing through Sara and she knew she had to ignore it. She couldn't spend the rest of her life like this.

'I'm not hungry.' She stood and pushed her chair in. 'Leave the plates and scraps. I'll sort it out when I come back tomorrow to look at your finger. You look much better. For a while there I thought we were going to have to go back to the hospital.'

Matt frowned. 'It's getting dark. I'm not happy about you going across the river in the dark.' He glanced up at the clock on the wall. 'And the tide will have turned. It's going out and it'll be flowing fast.'

Sara bit her lip. Matt was right; she hadn't thought about it being dark when she went back. 'True,' she agreed.

'Stay the night. There's plenty of spare rooms these days.' Matt stood and as he did, he put his hand to his head.

Sara reached out to him. 'What's wrong. Are you ill again?

'Just a bit dizzy when I stood up.'

'Okay. It's probably best that there's someone here with you. How the heck did your mother cope when she had four small children!'

'There was a bridge back in those days.'

'Okay. I think you should go back to bed. Have you had enough to eat?'

'Probably too much.'

'Do you . . . um . . . need a hand to wash or anything?'

'Or anything?' Despite his dizziness Matt's smile was cheeky.

He grabbed her hand and pulled her closer, unable to resist.

'Blame it on the fever.' He lowered his head and Sara widened her eyes as she realised his intention. Before she could move away, Matt's lips captured hers. His hand was gentle on her waist as he kissed her softly, and before she could respond he lifted his head, and his eyes were shadowed.

'Good night, Sara. We'll talk in the morning. Honesty deserves honesty back.'

Chapter Fifteen

Matt slept deeply and dreamlessly. He was woken at first light by the sound of his phone ringing. He reached over to the bedside table before he realised he'd left it in the kitchen. Pulling on his jeans over his boxers he padded softly down to the kitchen.

Sara was already there, sitting at the table; she was dressed, and her usually wild curls were neatly tied back.

'You're up early. Did my phone wake you?'

'No, I was already awake. I was coming to check on you and then go across river before the tide starts going out.' She gestured to his phone on the table. 'Your phone rang but I didn't like to answer it.' She seemed tense, and he worried about last night. He shouldn't have kissed her, but he'd been unable to resist.

'Yes, it woke me up. Excuse me for a moment.' Matt picked up his phone and looked at the time. It was still before six a.m. There was a missed call from Jake.

Strange.

He turned to Sara. 'Would you like to make us a cuppa before you go? I just have to make a call.'

151

'Is everything okay?'

'I hope so.'

As Sara filled the electric kettle, Matt returned Jake's call and Jake picked up instantly.

'Jake, you call—'

'Matt.' Jake's voice was quiet. 'We need you.'

'What's wrong?'

Sara lifted her head and looked at him and Matt stared at her as he listened to Jake, and his blood ran cold.

'Have you called the others?'

'Yes, they're on their way.'

'What about Mum?' Matt asked.

'I don't know what to do there.'

'Okay, we'll talk about it. Jake, I'm on my way. Stay calm, mate.'

He put the phone down and took a deep breath. 'Don't worry about the kettle, Sar. I'm going to get my shirt and shoes. We have to go to the hospital.'

'What's happened?' Sara crossed to him and stood close.

'It's Jenni.' Matt's voice cracked and he swallowed. 'She was ill through the night and complained of a severe headache. Jake couldn't rouse her this morning. He called triple zero and she's at the hospital. He needs someone to look after the children. It looks like the RFDS might fly her to Mt Isa. They're on the way now.'

'Let's go.' Sara switched the kettle off. 'Get a shirt and whatever you need. Do you want me to lock up?'

'No, it'll be fine.'

'I'll wait for you at the gate.' She picked up her purse and was out the back door as Matt ran up to his room and grabbed a shirt and his wallet. His thongs were at the back door— they'd do.

**

The sky was beginning to lighten, and scudding clouds ran across the half moon. The wind whistled eerily through the mangroves and the mournful cry of a plover reached them from the point.

'Are you okay to steer in this wind?' Matt asked as Sara climbed into the boat.

She was a little nervous, but more worried about Jenni. She nodded.

'Yes, I'm fine.'

Matt was in the boat and sitting on the front seat before she could even offer to help him in. His face was grim, and he stayed quiet as she steered them across the river.

'Pull in at the co-op,' he said. 'My ute's there and the keys are under the seat. It'll be quicker.'

Sara did as he instructed and was at the side of the boat ready to help him up on the higher wharf on this side of the river. He gripped her hand firmly but let go as soon as he was steady on his feet.

153

'Thank you.'

They ran to the ute and Matt opened the driver's door and went to jump in. Sara didn't say anything; it was only a block to the hospital, and he could steer one-handed.

'I'll put it in drive,' she said. 'Tell me when you're ready.'

He started the engine and nodded; she slid the shift into drive. It was only a minute or so before Matt parked in the small car park outside the medical surgery.

'I'll come around and open the door. Just wait,' Sara instructed.

She opened the door for him, and Matt took her hand as they hurried into the hospital. The main door was unlocked, and a woman was sitting on the seat nursing a baby. A little girl was playing with the toys in the corner of the waiting room. She looked up, her tired face lined with wrinkles and Sara realised it was Maisie who she'd last seen in the Barossa Valley.

Matt touched Maisie gently on the shoulder before he walked over and picked up the little girl.

'How's the prettiest girl in the universe?'

'Uncle Mattie.' The little girl planted kisses on Matt's cheek. He smiled but Sara knew it was hard for him.

'My Mummy's sick.'

154

'I know, sweetheart. The doctors will look after her.' He crouched down beside her as he put her back down near the toys and stayed there as she picked up a puzzle.

'Hello, Sara,' Maisie said quietly. 'I didn't realise you'd arrived.'

'I've been here a couple of days,' Sarah said. 'I start at the medical practice next week. Has the doctor seen Jenni yet?' Sara didn't like to go in. It wasn't the right thing to do.

'Doc Rose is with her now. And Jake. The poor guy is a mess. I'm just so pleased he thought to call me. I'm only a hundred yards down the road. I met him when he followed the ambulance in his car.'

The door opened and Sara looked up as Caro walked in.

The doctor's eyes widened in surprise when she saw Sara sitting next to Maisie. 'Sara. I'm pleased you're here. Can you wash up and come in, please? Hector called me and I stopped in at the motel to collect you.'

'I was over at Matt's. He wasn't well last night so I stayed to keep an eye on him.' Sara sensed Maisie's curiosity but didn't explain any further.

Caro stood and went over to Matt and their conversation was quiet. Maisie looked down and rocked the baby who was asleep in her arms. The mood in the room was sombre.

Sara followed Caro into the hospital. 'Why did you need me? '

'Hector asked if you would go on the plane with Jenni to Mt Isa.'

Sara nodded. 'Of course.'

'Her husband will be there too, and you can monitor her vital signs.'

'It's not an RFDS plane?

'No, it's the air ambulance from Mt Isa. They were short-staffed, and I said either you or I would go with Jenni. Do you need to get anything? It'll be here shortly.'

'No. I'm fine. I've got my phone in my bag. I don't need anything else.'

Caro reached over and squeezed her hand as they headed for the sink. They could hear Dr Rose's quiet voice coming from the end of the room.

'Hector suspects meningitis, but until the bloods come back and they do a spinal tap, we won't be sure.'

'Is she very bad, Caro?' Sara kept her voice quiet.

Caro sighed. 'It's not looking good.'

Sara's eyes filled and she blinked away the tears. 'I knew she wasn't well on Saturday when I saw her.'

'Don't beat yourself up. No one could have known this would happen. Jake did the right thing. He called triple zero.'

As they stood there a plane flew low over the hospital. 'There it is now. Hector wants to see you before you go.'

Sara nodded. In less than an hour, the lives of the McDougal family had been thrown into turmoil, and she prayed that Jenni would recover.

She was loved by so many people.

Chapter Sixteen

Jenni's battle was long, and she was still in danger three days later when Mum and Rick arrived in Mt Isa.

Matt's finger was healing—Sara had met him at the hospital twice to dress it and had kept him up to date on his sister's condition. On Thursday morning she'd called into the house where Maisie and Matt were staying with the children. After she left, Matt sat at the table with his head in his hands. Caro said Jenni still wasn't responding.

'They're doing all that they can, Matt, but she may have to be airlifted to Brisbane.'

'Uncle Mattie!' Leni's screech around midnight on Thursday night pulled him out of his thoughts, and he ran down the hall to the little girl's room, but Maisie was already there.

They had been a strange duo, caring for the children, but Maisie had been a trooper. Dane and Nicole had been delayed by the bad weather that had closed in just after the air ambulance had taken off for Mt Isa. Jenni had been extremely lucky to get there.

Donny and Claire had arrived and stayed with them at Jake and Jenni's house for one night before they all agreed it would be best if they went down to the Isa to be there for Jake.

Matt hadn't spoken to Sara and he'd tried not to think about her; they had bigger problems to deal with. For the first time, he was beginning to wonder if his determination to stay alone was the right path to follow.

It was not the time to think about it, but he missed her dreadfully. He hadn't seen Sara since she'd left the waiting room at the hospital. Just a brief glimpse as they'd wheeled Jenni out to the plane. Jake had run in and hugged each of the children before he left.

Matt had enveloped him in a hug as Jake had walked out with tears running down his face. 'Look after my sister, mate. Tell her I love her.'

Jake had nodded and hurried out.

Now Matt picked up Leni and held her close. The sweet smell of his sister's little girl almost brought him to tears. He'd never thought he wanted a family, but the events of this week had given him a whole new perspective on life.

When it was over—and he prayed that Jenni would come home well—Matt had decided to go outback. It was where he had done his best thinking years ago, and it was where he was going to go when this was all over.

159

The co-op had been shut all week, and in the scheme of things, it didn't matter. He had some big decisions to make.

His breath hitched as Leni's lips brushed his cheek. 'Don't be sad, Uncle Matt. Mummy just got better. I dreamed'd it.'

'That's lovely, sweetheart.' Matt's voice was thick.

Maisie looked at him as his phone rang in his pocket and she held her arms out for the little girl.

Matt's breath hitched as he looked at Jake's caller ID, and he walked into the hall. He hadn't spoken to Jake for three nights, Donny had been keeping them informed, each time there was a change in Jenni's condition. Unfortunately, she had deteriorated over the past twenty-four hours.

'Jake?'

Matt closed his eyes at the silence at the other end of the phone, and then there was the harsh sound of Jake crying.

His world fell to pieces around him as he waited. 'Jake? Tell me.'

***

Sara's phone rang at midnight as she tried to sleep. She had a room in the nurses' wing of Mt Isa Hospital. Jake had refused to leave the hospital. For a moment she thought it might be Matt; he hadn't called, and she didn't think it was right to call him when the family was so worried. There would be time one day to see what he wanted to be honest about. She reached for the phone and listened.

A moment later she was pulling her clothes on and running to the intensive care ward.

Helen and Rick met her at the door of the waiting room; they had arrived this afternoon, and the family had invited Sara to meet them for coffee in the hospital dining room, but Jake had stayed with Jenni.

Tears ran down Helen's face as she reached for Sara. Donny and Claire were sitting near the door. Donny held Claire close.

'Oh, Sara.'

Sara hugged the older woman as she clung to her.

Chapter Seventeen

Two days later Sara was on her way back to Normanton. Matt's mother, Helen and her partner, Rick, had booked a flight and had insisted that she accompany them.

'It's the least we can do, Sara,' Helen had said. 'You've been an amazing support to the family. And not only as a nurse but as a friend.'

As they waited for the plane in the small regional airport, Sara scrolled through the many text messages that she'd ignored over the past week. One message brought a smile to her face.

Helen looked at her. 'Good news?'

Sara nodded. 'I am now the almost owner of Mrs Plummer's house in Rosedale Street. My offer has been accepted.'

'That's another cause for celebration.'

'It is. I'll have a high tea and you're all invited. As soon as Jenni is well enough.'

Jenni's recovery from bacterial meningitis had been nothing short of a miracle. She had regained consciousness just before eleven o'clock that night, and her temperature had dropped almost to normal within an hour. Jake had been with her when she had opened her eyes and smiled at him and asked where the children were.

'That's wonderful news,' Helen said. 'So, you're staying? Your grandmother will be pleased.'

'She will,' Sara said. Helen had not mentioned Matt at all.

Dane picked them up at Normanton and hugged Sara. 'It's good to see you Sara, it's been a long time.'

'Too long, Dane. But I'm home now.'

Dane walked over and hugged Helen and then pulled her aside for a quiet word.

All Sara heard was him say. 'He just said he needed to get away.'

'That boy,' Helen muttered.

Sara had hoped that Matt would be waiting for them, but there was no sign of him when Dane dropped her at the motel.

'Sara, we'd love you to join us for dinner tonight if you're not too tired?'

Sara nodded shyly. 'If you're sure. I don't want to intrude.'

'Don't be silly. Come to the hotel about six.'

She waved as the car drove off and headed back to the brown room of the hotel.

Her phone rang before she had the door open.

'Welcome home, Sara. How about a coffee when you're settled?'

Sara looked around the depressing room. 'I've got a better idea. How about you bring your car and help me move?'

Caro obliged and by mid-afternoon, they were sitting at the table in Sara's soon-to-be-house sipping tea out of fine bone china. One of the cupboards had been full of china and ornaments and Sara hadn't been able to resist.

'I love this house, Sara. I can see you settled here for a long time.' Caro looked at her from beneath her lashes. 'Have you talked to Matt yet?'

'No. I . . . um . . . I thought I might go over to the co-o before it closes and say hello.'

Caro shook her head. 'The co-op's still not open. Hector told me Matt's gone away for a while.'

Shock ran through Sara. 'Away? Before Jenni comes home?

Caro nodded. 'Apparently. His brother is going to open the co-op on the weekend, and his sister-in-law is taking over looking after the kids. They seem like a lovely family. Very close.'

'They are. I wonder where Matt's gone.'

'You're still in love with him, aren't you?' Caro reached over and touched Sara's arm.

She nodded. 'Silly me. I am. And I think he knows it. That's probably why he fled town. Before I could come back and make a fool of myself.'

'I doubt it. I saw the way he looked at you. He cares about you, Sara.'

'He may care about me, but he doesn't love me.' Her breath hitched and she bit back the next words before she made a fool of herself.

Unlovable Sara.

'Don't give up. Fight for him.'

Sara shook her head sadly. 'You can't make someone love you.' She jumped to her feet. 'Come on, let's get this unpacking finished and then I'm going out for dinner. Do you want to come? I'm sure the McDougals wouldn't mind.'

Caro shook her head and her smile was secretive. 'I already have a date.'

Sara's mouth dropped open and she shut it quickly. 'A date? Who with?'

Caro blushed as Sara looked at her. 'Dr Hector Rose.'

Chapter Eighteen

Matt's finger ached as he lifted the swag out of his ute. Dr Caro had been insistent that she tape his finger up seeing he was going out of town for a few days.

'You keep it clean, Matt, and keep taking those antibiotics as a precaution.'

'Yes, doc,' he'd said.

He'd gotten sick of explaining why he was going away. All he'd say was that he needed some space. Caro insisted on knowing exactly where he was going.

'The last thing your family needs now is another incident.'

He'd told her his destination, but no one could talk him out of going away.

Matt needed to do some deep soul searching, and he had a favourite spot up the coast north of Jenni and Jake's house. His own outback paradise.

Jenni's illness had thrown him for a sixer, and he had begun to realise how short and tenuous life could be.

He'd been wasting time, and it was time to make some hard decisions. He needed to get away where he could think, and not be distracted.

The clearing was well away from the side of the small river that wound in from the west. He checked around for snakes, and then set to gathering firewood—with his left hand. It was surprising how he'd learned to do so many things left-handed over the past week.

By the time the sun had set, Matt was leaning against a log in front of a crackling fire. He stared into the flames and waited for his dinner to heat up in the camp oven hanging from the tripod above the flames. Maisie had insisted on cooking him a couple of meals to take away; she was the only one who'd understood why he wanted to get away and think.

One night after Jenni's two kids had gone to sleep, Maisie had offered him a wine and Matt had shaken his head.

'Thanks, Maisie. I don't drink.'

She'd nodded and sat back on the sofa. 'Unusual for a bloke up here.'

He pulled a face. 'I have my reasons. Or reason.'

'Over indulged once, did you?' she persisted.

'No. I've never drunk at all. Let's say I had my fill watching my father as I grew up. And I don't want to be like him.'

Maisie sat up straight. 'Matt McDougal! If you think you're anything like your father, you need to forget that quick smart. Bloody hell.' She shook her head. 'I'm going to have to go outside and have a ciggie.'

When she came back inside, she stood in front of Matt and wagged her finger. 'I knew your father. He played poker with my husband. Trust me, Matt, you don't have anything of him in you. Please believe me.'

'I don't want to find out the hard way. That's why I don't drink.'

'You think it was the drink that made him that way? I know he was your father, Matt, but believe me, he was a cold, mean man. Sober or drunk. It wasn't the drink, it was the way he was. Your mother deserved a medal living with him and putting up with his shit.'

'Thank you, Maisie. That means a lot to me.'

She flopped onto the sofa beside him and picked up her wine glass. 'Now you can have a social drink and enjoy it!'

##

Matt stood on the edge of the ridge and looked out over the valley. In the far distance, the Gulf glinted silver. The vegetation was a mix of beautiful purple and blues and he took in a deep breath. He walked back to his campsite and reached into the small esky that he'd brought with him.

It was a test.

In it was a six-pack of beer on ice he'd picked up at the IGA on the way out of town. He lifted out the first bottle, still cold from the ice around it and popped the top,

He put it to his lips and drank a mouthful. Putting the bottle on the ground beside him, Matt tilted his head back and waited for the sun to set. An hour later he was still looking at the sky and thinking, but now there were brilliant stars above.

Sara would be back in town, and he wanted to have his path of action very clear in his mind before he spoke to her.

He picked up the bottle, took a few mouthfuls and waited.

The stars twinkled above, the fire crackled, the aroma of Maisie's beef stew surrounded him, and Matt didn't feel any different. Maybe a little bit more relaxed. He waited for the anger and the frustration to kick in. And maybe a bit of mean.

But all he could think of was how happy he was that Jenni was on the road to recovery, and Sara was staying in Second Chance Bay.

With a shrug, he picked up the bottle and finished the beer.

If he was honest, he didn't even like the taste very much. A grin spread on his face as he thought how ridiculous he was being.

What had he expected?

To have a transformation like the Hulk? To have his muscles bulge and pop out of his shirt?

Matt McDougal, you're a moron.

He opened the esky and picked up another beer before he lifted the lid of the camp oven and stirred the stew that was now bubbling away.

It was serene out here. No lights, just the stars above and the wind in the trees. One day he would bring Sara to his secret spot.

Matt swallowed; his decision had been made for him by his heart—and maybe his common sense and a bit of Maisie wisdom thrown into the mix.

He had a lot to be thankful for. It didn't matter that his father had been a violent man. Jenni was recovering, he was part of a warm and loving family, his mother was happy, and if he was right, a cute and quirky woman with red curls had some feelings for him.

Before he could think about it anymore, Matt popped the top off the second beer and held it up to the sky.

Here's to my future. A future with Sara in it.

Well, you idiot, why are you out here in the scrub by yourself, while she's back in town?

As Matt pondered rolling up the swag and packing up camp, the sound of a car coming down the bush track caught his attention. He sat up straight and frowned.

A few minutes later, a truck with McDougal Fishing Charters written on the side pulled up at the side of his camp.

As though he was expecting them, his two younger brothers jumped down from the cabin and sauntered over. They looked at the beer in his hand and then both looked at each other.

'Having a party out here by yourself, are you, big bro?' Dane reached into the esky and pulled out two beers, threw one to Donny and then popped the top of the other.

'What are you two doing out here? And how did you find my secret spot?' he spluttered.

'Secret? Jeez, we used to come out here when we were kids. We've come to talk some sense into you, mate,' Donny said.

'And we've got something for you,' Dane added. 'Mum told us to bring you a present.'

'I don't need any sense talked into me. I've come to them by myself.'

'Does it involve a certain young woman?' Donny wiped the back of his hand over his mouth.

'It might,' Matt replied with a grin.

'About bloody time you got some sense into you.' Dane sniffed the air. 'That smells pretty good. Do you think we should stay for dinner, Donny?'

'Nah, we've both got a lovely woman waiting at home.'

'Not like this idiot.' Dane gestured with his head to Matt.

'Hey, watch it. So, what did you come out here for? What's this present Mum sent out?'

Matt shook his head as his two younger brothers walked to the truck and high-fived each other before they climbed into the truck.

'Mad bastards,' he muttered. 'But I do love the pair of you.'

The truck engine flared into life but before the large vehicle pulled away, a door slammed, and Matt looked up.

He squinted and then rubbed his eyes as the truck disappeared into the distance.

'Hello, Matt.' Sara's voice was soft as she held out a parcel wrapped in Alfoil. 'Your Mum sent me out with the bread to go with the stew that Maisie made for you.'

Matt's mouth opened and closed as he stared at her. For the first time ever, he was lost for words.

Sara walked over and put the bread on the ground beside the fire before she moved closer to him. She lifted her hand and put it on his heart.

'Matt? A few days ago, before Jenni got sick, you were about to be honest with me. It seems your whole family and half the town know something we don't. Is it a good time to tell me what you were going to say that night?'

Matt nodded and looped his arms around her slim waist. Her eyes were bright as she looked up and held his gaze.

'It is. I've known this for eight years, or more, but I was a coward. I'm so very sorry that I took all those years away from us. I was about to pack up and come to town and find you to tell you.'

'Tell me what, Matt?' Sara's soft lips were a rosy pink in the firelight as she whispered the words. Her breath warmed his mouth and Matt inched closer.

'I knew I loved you, and I knew even then I wanted you in my life, but I made a huge mistake. I was scared I was my father, and I didn't want to risk that with you.'

Sara's lips moved closer to his. 'You are Matt McDougal. No one else, and I love you just as you are. With your fears, and with your uncertainty, you have to know I love you unconditionally.'

'I love you, Sara Sweeney, and I always have. And I always will.' He looked over at the swag. 'Maybe it's just as well I packed the double swag?'

'Maybe it is.' Sara's lips widened in a sweet smile as she lifted her face for his kiss. Matt closed his eyes and breathed in her scent before he slid his mouth gently over her soft cheek, slowly making his way to those lips.

The night was silent around them and the stars smiled down as Matt kissed Sara properly for the first time in years. She lifted her head a fraction before he deepened the kiss.

'It was worth the wait, my darling Matt.'

Epilogue

The spring afternoon was filled by soft cloud, and the whisper of gentle rain was carried on the slight wind. Sara didn't care what the weather was like as Claire and Nicole fussed about her and straightened her dress.

'Mercy me, girl, aren't you ready yet?' Maisie burst into the room at the back of Mrs Plummer's—now Sara's—house. 'You don't want him to change his mind. He's standing under the tree in the backyard, pulling at his tie as if it's choking him.'

'Matt won't go anywhere,' Sara said with a smile. 'And I think we're ready, aren't we, girls?'

Nicole and Claire smiled and nodded. 'We are.'

'Well, what are you waiting for?' Maisie said.

They walked down the back stairs and Sara's heartbeat quickened as she saw Matt, flanked by his brothers and his brother-in-law, standing at the end of the garden. Jenni was sitting in a chair at the bottom of the steps, and as Sara reached her, Jenni held up her hand and took Sara's. Sara leaned over and kissed her cheek.

'Are you ready, Jen?'

Jenni nodded and stood, walking between Nicole and Claire. 'I wouldn't miss this for the

175

world. I've waited a long, long time to see my big brother happy.'

The strains of a slow love ballad floated on the air as the four girls walked towards their men. Jenni's two children waited at the front, each holding a basket of petals.

Helen and Rick, and Sara's Nan, sat proudly in the front row, beside Hector and Caro. Sara took another step towards her future and smiled when she saw the doctors' hands clasped together. Dan and Marcy sat in the row behind them; they'd become good friends over the past three months since Sara had arrived in town.

The family members and the other guests and the awareness of her surroundings left Sara as she took the last steps towards the man waiting for her.

The man who loved her.

Matt held out his hands and she lifted her eyes to his as a wave of love suffused her. His eyes held hers unwaveringly and the connection between them was as strong as though it was bound by one of the ribbons floating on the children's petal baskets.

'I love you, Sara,' Matt mouthed over the music as it swelled to a crescendo.

He held out his hand and entwined his fingers through hers as the celebrant began to speak.

'And I love you, Matt,' she whispered.

THE END

I hope you've enjoyed the Second Chance Bay series.

Try Annie's new series: The Augathella Girls

OTHER BOOKS from ANNIE

Whitsunday Dawn
Undara
Osprey Reef
East of Alice

Porter Sisters Series

Kakadu Sunset
Daintree
Diamond Sky
Hidden Valley
Larapinta
Kakadu Dawn

Pentecost Island Series
Pippa
Eliza
Nell
Tamsin
Evie
Cherry
Odessa
Sienna
Tess
Isla

The Augathella Girls Series
Outback Roads

Outback Sky
Outback Escape
Outback Wind
Outback Dawn
Outback Moonlight
Outback Dust
Outback Hope
An Augathella Surprise
An Augathella Baby
An Augathella Spring

Sunshine Coast Series
Waiting for Ana
The Trouble with Jack
Healing His Heart
Sunshine Coast Boxed Set

The Richards Brothers Series
The Trouble with Paradise
Marry in Haste
Outback Sunrise
Richards Brothers Boxed Set

Bondi Beach Love Series
Beach House
Beach Music
Beach Walk
Beach Dreams
The House on the Hill

Second Chance Bay Series
Her Outback Playboy
Her Outback Protector

ANNIE SEATON

Her Outback Haven
Her Outback Paradise
The McDougalls of Second Chance Bay Boxed Set

Love Across Time Series
Come Back to Me
Follow Me
Finding Home
The Threads that Bind
Love Across Time 1-4 Boxed Set

Bindarra Creek
Worth the Wait
Full Circle
Secrets of River Cottage
A Clever Christmas
A Place to Belong

Four Seasons Short and Sweet
Ten Days in Paradise
Follow the Sun

Others
Deadly Secrets
Adventures in Time
Silver Valley Witch
The Emerald Necklace
Christmas with the Boss
Her Christmas Star
An Aussie Christmas Duo (two Christmas novellas)

About the Author

2023: Winner of the long contemporary RUBY award for *Larapinta*

Finalist for the NZ KORU award 2018 and 2020.

Winner ...Best Established Author of the Year 2017 AUSROM

Long listed for the Sisters in Crime Davitt Awards 2016, 2017, 2018, 2019

Finalist in Book of the Year, Long Romance, RWA Ruby Awards 2016 *Kakadu Sunset*

Winner ...Best Established Author of the Year 2015 AUSROM

Winner ...Author of the Year 2014 AUSROM
Best Established Author, Ausrom Readers' Choice 2017
Book of the Year (Whitsunday Dawn) Ausrom Readers' Choice Awards 2018